Adolph Paul Oppé

The new comedy

Adolph Paul Oppé

The new comedy

ISBN/EAN: 9783337103583

Printed in Europe, USA, Canada, Australia, Japan

Cover: Foto ©Andreas Hilbeck / pixelio.de

More available books at **www.hansebooks.com**

University of St. Andrews

GRAY PRIZE ESSAY

THE NEW COMEDY

BY

A. P. OPPÉ

ἀπ' αἰγείρου θέα

ST. ANDREWS

W. C. HENDERSON AND SON

UNIVERSITY BOOKSELLERS

1897

Edinburgh : T. and A. CONSTABLE, Printers to Her Majesty

PREFACE

If, within this essay itself, there does not appear to be enough justification for grouping the Middle and the New Comedies under one head, its value is half destroyed. Yet it is worth recording that the distinction, as held until recently, is not mentioned by any one before the age of Hadrian. For, besides the anonymous authorities quoted in the essay, the Middle Comedy is unknown to the earlier Alexandrians, to Quintilian, to Velleius, to Harpocratio, to Dorotheus Ascalonita, to Plutarch, and to the Roman grammarians who lived before the death of Trajan.

This seems to have been shown first by Fielitz (*de attica comoedia bipartita*, Bonn, 1866), and to have been adopted by Dénis (*Comédie grecque*, Paris, 1886), neither of which books have I been able to procure. It was adopted by Theodor Kock in his monumental edition of the Fragments (Leipzig, 1884-1888), and almost convinces Maurice Croiset (A. & M. Croiset, *Litt. gr.*, vol. iii., Paris, 1891), who, however, retains the old arrangement because it is 'commode.' Otto Crusius attacked Kock fiercely in *Philologus* (xlvi) because of his innovation, but, despite his italics and his reference to Didymus, he is not convincing. More value is there in the article of Kaibel (*Hermes*, 1889), who ascribes the bipartition to the Pergamene scholars, on the ground that they argued from style and language alone, while the tripartition, he considers, was Alexandrian. But similarity of style is not the only reason for joining the Middle to the New Comedy.

I have not been able to refer in the essay to all the books which have helped me. The one I have followed most is the *Littérature Grecque* of M. Croiset. I have quoted the fragments everywhere by the numbers in Kock's edition. Other books referred to are :—

Historia Critica Comoediae Graecae,
Comicorum Graecorum Fragmenta, } A. Meineke
Menandri et Philemonis Reliquiae, Berlin.

Ménandre. Étude, Historique et Littéraire sur la Comédie et la Société Grecques, Guillaume Guizot; Paris, 1855.

Geschichte des Dramas, J. L. Klein; Leipzig, 1865.

Roman Poets of the Republic, W. Y. Sellar; Oxford, 1881.

The Attic Theatre, A. E. Haigh; Oxford, 1891.

Aristotle's Theory of Poetry and Fine Art, S. H. Butcher, 1895.

Athenaeus is quoted by the numbers and chapters of Dindorf's 1827 edition, and the Scholia on Aristophanes are from his 1822 edition.

I have added an Appendix in which will be found most of the passages, in the ancient commentaries, to which I have referred in the essay. They are quoted by the numbers attached to them in vols. i. and ii. of Meineke, *Fragmenta Comicorum Graecorum.*

CONTENTS

6   CONTENTS

THE NEW COMEDY

I.—THE END OF THE OLD COMEDY

It is characteristic of the early grammarians that they laid down distinctions for their own convenience, which prove the greatest difficulties to scholars of a later age. Thus, in the history of Greek Comedy, troubled by a period of transition between the old and the new, the grammarians of the age of Hadrian carelessly, but firmly, marked off an intermediate class—the middle. It is a careless distinction, because a settled date rarely marks the beginning or the end of an epoch of thought and literature, and a firm one, as has been proved by the laborious efforts of later scholars to reconcile the facts with the theories. However, before discussing the question of the Bipartition of Attic Comedy, it is necessary to see why the Old Comedy gave way to the Middle or the New.

The Old Comedy declined, and finally died with the period of Attic prosperity. But the grammarians, intent on some fixed reasons, had recourse to a law which would kill off the Old Comedy, either by suppressing the Chorus, and with it the *parabasis*, or by rendering the *parabasis* useless, taking away the *raison d'être* of the Chorus. Such laws, according to them, had been passed before, and some of these laws we find mentioned

in the Scholia on Aristophanes.   The earliest is the
one passed in the archonship of Morychides (440 B.C.),
which lasted two years, and was repealed in the archonship of Euthymenes.[1]   The scholiast tells us nothing
about this bill, except that it concerned comedy.

Again, in 416 a law forbidding personal burlesque
was passed by Syracosius, according to the testimony
of a scholiast on Aristophanes' *Birds*,[2] who quotes
Phrynichus in support of his statement.   In this case
it is much more probable that the fragment of Phrynichus gave rise to this belief in the law itself, though
the hopelessly corrupt state of the scholium does not
allow us to be certain on either side.   Yet the supposi-
tion that this law is merely a figment of the scholiast
to explain a passage in the *Birds* and the fragment of
Phrynichus is much strengthened by another instance.
In the *Acharnians*, which was produced in 425 B.C.,
Aristophanes mentions a certain Antimachus, who,
when he was choregus, did not invite to the usual
dinner, perhaps the poet himself, perhaps the whole
chorus.   Here [3] the scholiast notes that Antimachus
had carried a law to the effect that no one was to be
ridiculed by name in comedy, and that by doing so
he caused many of the poets not to bring out plays.
Therefore, says the scholiast, many of the chorus were
in want, and, he adds, Antimachus was choregus when
he brought forward the bill.

This story is clearly a fable, since, firstly, we have
no evidence of a change of the character of comedy

---

[1] Schol. Ar. *Ach.* 67 ; App. 1.
[2] Schol. Ar. *Av.* 1297 ; App. 3.   For the possible influence of
Alcibiades on Syracosius, cf. Meineke, *H.C.C.Gr.*, p. 40, and App. 4.
[3] Schol. Ar. *Ach.* 1150 ; App. 2.

about this time. In fact, the *Acharnians* itself belongs
to the period when personal satire was at its height;
and, secondly, even if the plays had changed slightly,
and become like the *Birds*, then the chorus would still
be in as important a position as it was before. Nor is
it probable that the scholiast refers to the law of 440;
he is only trying to explain a somewhat obscure line by
the imperfect memory of things he had read elsewhere.
But the foolish ignorance and assumption of knowledge
shown by the scholiasts are equally well demonstrated
in another note on the name Antimachus,[1] where the
grammarian gives a list of the Antimachi known to
history, and names the one mentioned above as the
son of Ψακάς, and this, apparently, in all seriousness.

It would be useless to mount up the charges of
ignorance against the scholiasts. There are too many
well-known ones. Yet it is as well to mention the
confusion of the scholiast on the *Clouds*,[2] who states
that Aristophanes did not exhibit under his own name,
because it was unlawful for one under thirty (or forty)
years to read a play in the theatre or to speak in the
assembly. Here he is evidently thinking of the law
which prohibited a man under forty from exhibiting
a chorus of boys at the Dionysia.[3]

Passing over the law which prevented an Areopagite
from writing a comedy,[4] and the one against ridiculing
the archon,[5] we come to the law which was commonly
considered the deathblow of the Old Comedy. Cinesias we know, from several passages, to have been the

---

[1] *Clouds*, 1018.   [2] *Clouds*, 510-530; App. 6.
[3] Aristotle, Ἀθ. πολ., c. 56; Aeschines *in Timarchum*, § 11.
[4] Plutarch, *Bellone an pace praest. Athen.*, p. 348 c; App. 10.
[5] Schol. on Ar. *Clouds*, 31; App. 11.

constant butt of the comic poets, owing to his wretched dithyrambs and his extraordinary impiety. That he deserved this is probable, and is shown, to some extent, by the fragment of a speech of Lysias[1] against him, which recounts some of his actions, and mentions the fact that he was constantly abused by the comic poets. It would seem that he retaliated on his enemies by doing away with the Choregia, or, according to another scholium, by attempting to do so. But we have no evidence as to the date of this law beyond the fact that it was carried soon after the *Frogs* was produced.

Platonios (p. xxxiii) says that as long as the democracy was powerful, comedy attacking individuals was allowed and favoured, but when the oligarchy arose and the tyrants came, then men were afraid to attack openly, and so it came about that the comedy became quieter, and that such plays as the *Aeolosicon* of Aristophanes and the *Odysseis* of Cratinus were produced.[2] Another writer says that it was owing to Alcibiades that the change was made,[3] and he defines the change as that from open scurrility to hidden or αἰνιγματώδης satire.[4]

It is evidently not to a law which, like the law of Cinesias, deprived the plays of choruses, that they refer, for of the plays of Aristophanes the *Lysistrata* and the *Thesmophoriazusae* were brought out after 400, and the *Frogs* itself in 405, when Athens was on the point of being invested by the Spartans. All these

---

[1] Lysias, fr. 34, *apud Athenaeum*, 12, 551 d ; cf. Aristophanes *passim*.

[2] Most of the anonymous commentators are content with saying, briefly, that the change in comedy took place when wickedness had gained the upper hand in Athens.

[3] App. 4.   [4] App. 13.

plays have choruses, and it is therefore clear that before 405 Cinesias had not succeeded in carrying through his bill. If he did succeed soon after, it was in the time of the Thirty, or in the newly re-established democracy. However, in 388 we have the *Plutus* with the remainder of a chorus; and, unless there was a continual passing and repealing of these bills, it is impossible to find by what law the chorus was extinguished or at what time the law was in force, or, indeed, whether there was ever a law at all.

But a clue to the truth of the story of Cinesias is to be found in the note of the scholiast[1] himself. He says that Strattis, in a play named after Cinesias, and dealing with his impiety,[2] calls him χοροκτόνος, because he did away with the choruses of comedy. But since we know Cinesias to have been an atrociously bad dithyrambic poet, it is by no means impossible that the epithet refers more to his treatment of his own choruses than to that of choruses in general. And, if Cinesias forbade the κωμῳδεῖν ὀνομαστί, thereby putting an end to the chorus and the *parabasis*, it would have been impossible for Strattis to produce a play named after him.

There is also mention of a law of Agyrrhios in the scholium on Ar. *Eccl.* 102,[3] but, as it only says that he cut down the expenses of the chorus, it has no importance here.

We have then two classes of laws mentioned. One of them did away with the chorus, the other prohibited ridicule by name.[4] The first, we see, was not in force

---

[1] Schol. Ar. *Ran.* 404; App. 5.   [2] Harpocratio, p. 111, 25.

[3] App. 7.

[4] Horace, *A. P.* 283—' Lex est accepta chorusque Turpiter obticuit,

in 388, when the *Plutus* came out, for that play has still a chorus, and it is improbable that it was to evade the law that Aristophanes made his chorus 'a little one.' The second, if limited to a prohibition of introducing personages on the stage, and of the *parabasis,* is a possible one, and perhaps remained in force, since the later plays were probably more or less harmless in their personalities. But, even in the New Comedy, living personages are mentioned, and possibly were introduced [1] on the scene. Moreover, the writers on comedy scarcely mention these laws, with the exception of the one who not only makes Alcibiades duck Eupolis in the sea, but also makes him the author of a bill to prevent open ridicule.[2] Platonios and others merely state that a fear fell on the poets, as those who were ridiculed demanded satisfaction. It is therefore possible that there were cases of libel against the poets, and that this helped to make the κωμῳδεῖν ὀνομαστὶ impossible.

Again, Platonios [3] states that it was owing to the poverty of the people after the Peloponnesian war that the choregi were not appointed for comedies. This may be true for a few years, though it is improbable. Tragedy was still allotted choruses, and the men's and boys' dithyrambic choirs were still kept up.[4] Besides, we have no proof of a general impoverishment;[5] if there had been, it would have been merely temporary;

sublato jure nocendi'—is insufficient evidence when compared with facts.

[1] e.g. *Mnesiptolemos* of Epinicus.
[2] *Anon. apud Cramer,* l.c. ; App. 4.
[3] App. 8; Croiset, *Litt. Grec.,* iii. ch. xiii. p. 583.
[4] Ar. 'Αθ. πολ., ch. 56. Demosthenes *in Meidiam, passim.*
[5] Holm, *History of Greece,* vol. iii. ch. ii.

and, from our knowledge of the Athenian character, we know it to be unlikely that the people would suffer a loss of their own enjoyment, because they thought there were not enough rich men to pay for it. They would have extorted the liturgies for comedy sooner than for triremes, and would have preferred the complete bankruptcy of the rich to a loss of any of their rights.

We have, therefore, many indirect testimonies to the effect that the chorus was suppressed about the end of the fifth century. None of them are convincing, and the laws are highly improbable.[1] Yet the fact remains that, after the Peloponnesian war, Attic comedy lost its old character, and entered on a new course, which was to culminate in the plays of Menander. It is not in laws that we are to find the cause of this change, it is in the state of Athens and the comedy itself.

The Old Comedy was the tremendous outburst of a young people enjoying a relapse into a semi-barbaric condition. As long as Athens was supreme, or felt itself supreme, this was possible. The citizens were more interested in the State than in themselves, and certainly more touched by politics than by literature. In those days the great tragedies were being played in public, philosophy was only known to a certain *élite*, and literature was not intended to be read. But in the fourth century it is presumable that the plays of Aeschylus, Sophocles, and Euripides were read in private, and it is impossible that some echoes of the philosophic movements did not reach the people. The

---

[1] It is very noticeable that in none of the commentaries on comedy have we any mention of the increase of the number of comedies, at the Dionysia or Lenaea, from three to five. Ar. Aθ. πολ., c. 56; Arg. Ar. *Plutus*; *Inscrr.*; Haigh, *Attic Theatre*, p. 30.

city was turning from its creative mood to a critical one. The tragedians—even Euripides—were more intent upon what a play should be in form than that it should be good. Stage conditions were perfected, a life-likeness was studied, and, consequently, the larger humanity of the earlier artists was overlooked.

It is not surprising, then, that the episodic liveliness of Aristophanes should give way to a quieter and more sober ridicule of life and manners. Politics were now more important,—or became more important towards the middle of the century,—but, all the same, more tiresome. The people did not take enough interest in them in the Assembly to enjoy a travesty of them on the stage. The riot of the Old Comedy, too, descended to the law courts,[1] and in its place both Tragedy and Comedy accepted a rationalising, argumentative interest from the sophists and the orators.

In every direction, indeed, we see the creative faculty of the Athenians giving way to a purely critical one. After the war comes the period when Plato wrote his exquisite prose, and when oratory was striving to the ideal of Isocrates. The tragedians after Euripides were conspicuous for two qualities, that of oratorical drama[2] and that of well elaborated stage effects.[3] Comedy

---

[1] The instances of comic phraseology or ideas in Demosthenes are too frequent to need quotation. It will suffice to point out the passages where the orator refers to Meidias' house as darkening the surrounding country (xxi. 158), and where he mentions his birth in § 149.

[2] Critias was a tragedian famous for his oratorical speeches.—Croiset, iii. ch. viii. p. 369. Aphareus, Astydamas, Theodectus, were pupils of Isocrates.

[3] Aristotle, *Poetics*, notes several ἀναγνωρίσεις and περιπέτειαι of the new school, and mentions their want of ἤθη.—Croiset, *l.c.*

then could no longer remain, as it was before, a particular, if highly amusing, *revue* of the deeds of the year. Something more general in its application was required, something which would appeal to the population at large. This, coupled with the gradual degeneration of the chorus, culminating in tragedy with Agathon, gave rise to the comedies of the fifth century, whose only certain characteristics were the absence of the παράβασις and the probable absence of the chorus.[1] This absence of the chorus, due to the deterioration of the lyrical gift, and to its having little part in a softened comedy, had not its origin in a law, but was the result of an inevitable decay and of the change of ideas.

II.—THE SO-CALLED MIDDLE COMEDY

Whatever, then, were the causes of the change, whether it was due to the general softening of Athenian manners, to some pecuniary want of the people at large, or to a timidity as to the ridicule of prominent personages, comedy did change character about 403. About that time political personages were burlesqued under ficti-

---

[1] On the absence of chorus in the New Comedy.—The commentators who allow a law to have put an end to the Old Comedy of course recognise no chorus in (the Middle and) the New (Hor. *A. P.* l.c.). We have however some possible traces of one in the Στεφανοπώλιδες of Eubulus and the *Circe* of Anaxilas (Mein. *Hist. Cr. Com. Gr.*, p. 302), and in the Τροφώνιος of Alexis. But this is at least doubtful. The Δωδωνίς of Antiphanes may have had a chorus. Of the names of the plays, the surest test, in my opinion, the only ones I remember as being probable names of choruses, are the Ὧραι of Anaxilas and the Μῆνες of Philetaerus. Kock denies the possibility of the Πόλεις of Anaxandrides being a play like the old comedy. Nothing can be found in the fragments of any of these three plays to help a decision.

tious names, and about 388 the chorus was dead or
dying. The years between 388 and 336 were allotted
by scholars to the comedy called Middle, on the
authority of later grammarians. But it is impossible
to find any real reason why the comedy should be
divided into two parts by the date 336. On the contrary, it would be better to place the Middle Comedy,
if one were wanted, between 403 and 388. We find
authority for this in the writings of those commentators
on comedy who mention a middle stage.

Of these, most[1] state that Comedy was of three kinds—
first, the stage of open abuse ; second, the stage of hidden
satire ; and third, with no satire except of slaves and
strangers. The typical poet of the first class was
Cratinus ;[2] Aristophanes and Eupolis were partly of
the Old Comedy, and partly of the Middle, of which
the chief writer was Plato. Menander and Philemon
were typical of the New.

Of the others, Platonios (p. xxxiv) states that the
plays which had the characteristics of the Middle had
no chorus, no parabasis, no personalities, and no masks
made after the likeness of citizens. He cites, as instances, the *Acolosicon* of Aristophanes and the *Odysseis*
of Cratinus, which were parodies. Two commentaries[3]
name Aristophanes as the initiator of the New Comedy
with his *Cocalus* and *Plutus*; one of them is entirely

---

[1] *Anon. de Com.*, p. xxi fin. ; *Schol. Dion. Thrac. apud. Bekk. Anec.*,
p. 747 ; *Andronicus apud Bekk. Anec.*, p. 1461 ; *Anon. apud Cramer
Anecd. Paris*, p. 3 *seq.* ; *Tzetzes*, περὶ διαφορᾶς ποιητῶν, 75-86. Most
of these assign the change from the Middle to the New to a law,—their
usual resource in times of trouble ; App. 13.

[2] The names given as typical of the different ages of comedy disagree
slightly ; App. 13.

[3] App. 15.

ignorant of a middle age.[1] From these evidences it
is clear that the Old Comedy was at its height till
the end of the Peloponnesian war, that the Middle
lasted until the death of Plato and the production of
the *Plutus*, and that the New continued from this
date (388) to the end of the century, and even after
that.

As at present arranged the typical poet of the
Middle Comedy is Antiphanes. He and his contemporaries are said to be of the Middle Comedy by
Suidas, Athenaeus, and by others of the later age,[2]
who place Plato in the Old Comedy. It is easy to
see how this change arose. The older authorities
called the poets who did not bring living people on
the stage, but ridiculed them in a hidden way, the
Middle Comedy. This distinction not appearing
evident to later grammarians, they transferred the
name of Middle from the poets before 388 to those
of the new school who lived before Chaeronea.[3] Of
course, since the change from one period to another
is gradual, the Middle Comedy might be joined to the
Old in its later form, as well as to the New, had we no
evidence to decide the question. It is now necessary
to discuss this evidence.

The earlier poets of the fourth century wrote plays
which may be divided into the classes of Parody and
General Caricature. Of these, Parody was their distinctive feature, as compared with the later poets,

---

[1] App. 14.

[2] One of the Anon. on comedy, p. xxx (App. 16), but his definition
of the Middle Comedy of Antiphanes and Alexis will be examined
below.

[3] Kock, *Com. Frag. Att.*, vol. ii. Preface, who quotes Fielitz. See
Preface.

and the greatest link which joins them to the later
Old Comedy. But the parody of the old Comedy contained allusions to men of the time under the mythical
names. This explains the word αἰνιγματώδης, so constantly recurring in the commentaries on Comedy as an
epithet of the Middle group of poets. In the New
Comedy [1] these parodies were merely funny representations of the old tragic characters as ordinary people,
and we must remember that in later tragedy the heroes
acted more as ordinary people than as heroes. The
older tragedians felt the artistic necessity which commands a work of art not to tell a story. Their plots
were stories known to every one, and consequently of
little importance. Their whole duty was to draw a
picture of ἤθη, and to make it artistic, without
attempting to conciliate the audience by the interest
of exciting stories. The newer tragedians, depending
on their mastery over the accessories, made their personages human and ordinary, some introducing new
characters into old plays, others, like Agathon, using
no old action or character. It is easy to see how the
comic poets would treat these debased heroes of tragedy
and make them more ordinary still. Heracles, for
instance, we know from several fragments, was represented in the New Comedy, not as an orator ridiculed
symbolically for his public misdeeds, but as a glutton
and an ordinary Boeotian. These parodies will be
treated more fully in the part of the essay where the
plays of the New Comedy will be discussed at length.
Here it is sufficient to point out that it is not only in
Antiphanes, Eubulus, and Anaxandrides that we find

---

[1] Henceforth, except in dealing with other writers who use the term
Middle, I shall use the style New Comedy for all the poets after 388.

these plays on mythical subjects, there are also examples in Diphilus, Philemon, and Menander,[1] and we
have an example in the *Amphitruo* of Plautus. Therefore, if we have to draw a fixed line between the Middle
and the New Comedy, we cannot use the absence or
presence of these plays as a criterion. We can only
say with Meineke that Philemon and Diphilus were
occasionally poets of the Middle Comedy, and, *vice
versa*, when Antiphanes and his contemporaries wrote
plays with similar titles and fragments to those of
Menander, we can only use the meaningless phrase,
and say that these poets were in advance of their
age. That the art of parody declined in time is only
natural, but since it was only one of the subjects used,
it would be absurd to ignore the others and use it alone
as the test of the difference in Comedy.

This difference between the so-called Middle and the
New Comedy has been a source of trouble to most
writers on Greek literature. The later grammarians,
we see, were satisfied with the distinction, and gave
no reasons for it. Thus, the anonymous author Περὶ
κωμῳδίας (p. xxx) divides the middle and the new
into two classes, the first with Antiphanes and Alexis
as chief exponents, and the second with Menander and
Philemon.[2] He defines the Middle Comedy as devoid
of poetic form, and principally concerned with plots,
while of the New Comedy he gives no description whatever. This definition is, of course, just that which is
elsewhere given to the New Comedy as opposed to the

---

[1] Philemon wrote Μυρμιδόνες, Παλαμήδης, Χάριτες, though none of
these are certain mythological plays ; Menander, Δάρδανος, Ψευδηρα-
κλῆς, and perhaps the Λευκαδία is to be counted. Diphilus wrote five
or six ; Euphro, Θεῶν ἀγορά, Μοῦσαι ; Lynceus, Κένταυρος ; Philippides, Ἀμφιάρεως ; Timostratus, Πάν.   [2] App. 16.

the Old and outspoken comedy, and the Middle and
αἰνιγματώδης. If we allow the Middle Comedy to
have been better in form than the New, we at once
deprive the latter of its particular excellence, since we
should be obliged to admit that it was more sketchy
and episodic in character than the Middle. This, besides being contrary to the evidence of Plautus and
Terence, is opposed to the nature of evolution. For it
is natural that from the episodic politics of Aristophanes the next step would be to an episodic caricature
of manners, and the last and most perfect stage would
be the well-constructed plays which Aristotle notices,
and which Menander wrote. On the other hand, if the
Middle Comedy was really episodic when compared with
the New, it is hardly possible that the anonymous
writer would consciously give a definition to one, which
belongs particularly to the other.

But the anonymous writer is supported by the much
greater authority of Aristotle. Besides the passage in
the *Ethics*,[1] where he contrasts the αἰσχρολογία of the
Old Comedy with the ὑπόνοια of his contemporaries,
and which might be construed into a reference to the
hidden satire, we have many passages in the *Poetics*
which point conclusively to a comedy of intrigue in
his day. It is just the fact that Aristotle died
before Menander was born, which O. Crusius *tam alta
voce* considers the weak point in the appeal to his
authority,[2] that lends the greatest weight to the argument. For if intrigue had not become a regular part

---

[1] *Eth. Nic.* iv. 14.

[2] Crusius attacked Kock's bipartition of Attic Comedy in Philologus
xlvi. His chief argument was the death of Aristotle before Menander's
first production of a play.

of the comedy of his day, he would not have defined
the double turn of fortune as being the property of
comedy,[1] nor could he have spoken of the comic poets
as inventing their plots according to the probable, and
making them general, not particular.[2]

It is evident from this that Menander's ideal of
comedy was much that of Antiphanes, the difference
being only one of degree.   In fact it may be said that
Menander only perfected the work of the earlier poets,
and it would be absurd to class the best representatives
of a literary epoch as belonging to another.   The fact
that Aristotle's definition of comedy is carried out by
Menander, though it was laid down with reference to
his predecessors, constitutes a link between the two
ages which no battle of Chaeronea could destroy.

Again, writers on Greek literature have defined the
Middle Comedy (388-336) as being intermediate between the Old and the New in every characteristic.
Klein[3] says that its domain was limited on one side
by the ἀγορά, and on the other by the private house.
The plays of the Middle Comedy, therefore, were confined to the street and the palaestra, and, in general, to
semi-public life, while the New had for its material the
domestic life of the people.   This would be a convenient
distinction if it were true, but a glance at the facts will
show that it is unfounded.

---

[1] Ar. *Poet.* 1453 a: ἐστὶν δὲ οὐχ αὑτή (ἡ διπλῆ σύστασις) ἀπὸ τραγῳδίας
ἡδονὴ ἀλλὰ μᾶλλον τῆς κωμῳδίας οἰκεία.

[2] Ar. *Poet.* 1451 b: ἐπὶ μὲν οὖν τῆς κωμῳδίας ἤδη τοῦτο δῆλον γέγονεν·
(*i.e.* the generalising of poetry). συστήσαντες γὰρ τὸν μῦθον διὰ τῶν
εἰκότων, οὕτω τὰ (οὐ τά, Butcher) τυχόντα ὀνόματα ὑποτιθέασιν καὶ οὐχ
ὥσπερ οἱ ἰαμβοποιοὶ περὶ τὸν καθ' ἕκαστον ποιοῦσιν.   Cf. 1449 b.

[3] Klein, *Geschichte des Dramas*, ii. p. 208.   He carries out the
idea of a middle, class-satirising, intrigueless comedy, to its full ab-
surdity.   Cf. Guizot, *Ménandre* (Paris, 1855), pp. 166-172 and 216 *seq.*

It is true that the earlier poets wrote several plays to which they gave, as titles, the names of men, and, if it were lawful to bring on the stage public characters, and to give them principal parts in the play, it does not seem that these plays could have differed much from the Old Comedy. But apart from the statements that burlesque was αἰνιγματώδης, even in the later Old Comedy, we know that masks were not made in the likeness of men during the fourth century.[1] If an ordinary comic character were given a fancy mask, even if he, or she, were called by the name of some living personage, there would be little difference between him and a Chremes, of whom every member of the audience could find a dozen prototypes. Again, Aristotle is authoritative in this question, when he says that comedy was general, and not particular. The real nature of these plays, which were named after men, will be discussed in the proper place.

Yet, if the poets of the Middle Comedy were in the habit of introducing living people on the stage, so too were those of the New,[2] and in incidental remarks concerning public characters the New Comedy is almost as rich as the Middle. In regard to the Hetairae, Menander, as well as Antiphanes and Alexis, named plays after living courtesans, and, besides the fragments, Plautus and Terence show us that the hetaira was the stock subject of Comedy.

It is difficult, then, to understand why the Middle

---

[1] Pollux, *Onom.* iv. § 143; Platonios, p. xxxv; App. 12.

[2] Epinicus, Μνησιππόλεμος; Diphilus, Τελεσίας, Τιθραύστης, Ἀμαστρις; Posidippus, Μύρμηξ; Menander, Θαίς, Ὕμνις, Φαυλίον. Diphilus and Philemon—those poets approaching the Middle Comedy character—have no plays named after courtesans.

Comedy dealt more with the street and less with the home than the New. Nothing can be more domestic than the παρθένων φθοραὶ καὶ ἔρωτες, which Suidas attributes to Anaxandrides, while he calls him a poet of the Middle. These, which were the invention of Aristophanes, were the bases of the New Comedy plays, sharing, as we see in the Roman translations, the honours with those plots which turned on the purchase of a courtesan. The ὕλη of the New Comedy is all to be found in the Middle, where intrigue was probably less developed, and parodies were more plentiful. There is no certain difference such as there is between the plays before and after the year 400 B.C., so that, if we are to have a Middle Comedy, let it be in the time between (say) 403 and 388, when satire was no longer open, and intrigue had not commenced. With the Κώκαλος of Aristophanes, comedy entered into the period of general caricature and interesting intrigue, and from that time it has developed gradually and has never changed.

It is necessary, however, to glance at a class of play mentioned by historians of literature as distinctive of the Middle Comedy, and which I have not noticed. This is the class about γρῖφοι and riddle-guessers, which Meineke calls, for the sake of brevity, *Aenigmaticum*.[1] In this he seems to have been, consciously or unconsciously, led away by the recurrent αἰνιγματώδης of the anonymous writers. There can be no reason to believe

---

[1] Meineke, *Hist. Crit. Com. Gr.*, pp. 277, 278. The fragments containing riddles are *Antiph.* 124, 194,* 196* ; *Eubulus* 107* ; *Alexis* 240, 50 (cf. 103), *Athen.* x. ch. 69 *seq.*

The three marked with an asterisk have the riddle itself in hexameters.

that the Greeks ever went to the theatre to hear riddles
propounded on the stage, though it is only natural
that the poets did not overlook such an easy object of
comedy as the riddle-guesser.   From the important
position assigned by Meineke to these plays, one is led
to believe that Sappho, in the comedy of Antiphanes,
is only brought on the stage for the sake of exhibiting
her prowess in inventing and solving riddles.   But
Sappho is a common subject of comedy, and of one
play at least we can reconstruct a plot entirely removed
from all riddles.[1]   The *Cleobulina* of Alexis probably
only introduced some woman who made riddles, like the
Παροιμιαζόμενος of Antiphanes, who was, in the words
of Kock and Meineke, 'homo Sanchonis Pansae vel
Sam Welleri instar,' or the *Phileuripides* of Philippides,
who must have been a man of sententious commonplace
and quotation, possibly Philemon.   What was the
place of these characters in the intrigue we can only
guess, but there is nothing particular to the Middle
Comedy in the ridicule of any one class of characters.
If the New Comedy rejected the Riddle-Guesser, it
kept the whole list of characters known to us by the
fragments, the plays of Plautus, and the notes on masks
of Pollux.

III.—THE DOMESTIC DRAMA

In attempting to reconstruct the most prominent of
the classes of plays written in the fourth century, the
Domestic Plays, it is well to begin with a consideration
of the characters who appeared on the scene.   It has

---

[1] Diphilus, Σαπφώ.

already been noted that these characters were typical, as opposed to the individual figures of the Old Comedy as we know it. It was the object of the New Comedy playwright to amuse the public by representing certain characters, whose qualities were at once obvious to the audience, and to manipulate them in the shifting scenes. Originally, perhaps, the poets were content with placing the characters on the stage as puppets to be laughed at, for their peculiar evolutions. But it soon became necessary to construct a continuous plot which would be interesting of itself, and would give play to the actors. These plots will be discussed afterwards, but since these characters were so well defined, and took such a ready position in the scenes, they must be described first.

Nearly all the plays must have contained young men of a class which was probably common at Athens. They were idle and spendthrift, the natural result of an education that led to no purpose. They were, of course, always falling in love, and being restrained by their fathers who were avaricious, or being humoured by fathers who were careless. These are stock characters, and, in themselves, unobjectionable. The poet does not say that all Athenian youths were of this class, but, from the very nature of the play, they were necessary. A more virtuous youth who led an even life would be nearly useless for purposes of dramatic intrigue.

The other characters, however, are more informing as to the nature of the New Comedy. The parasite[1]

---

[1] The *locus classicus* for parasites is Athenaeus vi. c. 28 *seq.* In Diphilus 116 one calls himself μέλας, which is a reference to the black dress they always wore on the stage. Pollux 4. 119 : οἱ δὲ παράσιτοι μελαίνῃ ἢ φαιᾷ (ἐσθῆτι ἐχρῶντο).

was an easy object of caricature, invented, it is said, by Epicharmus. How he arose we cannot know, nor what was his position in Athenian society. He may have been the outcome of the sycophant who had left the service of the State, and was ready to enrol himself as an auxiliary to any family of wealth. But he is more probably merely an evolved form of the greedy hanger-on, who would have a natural place in a rude comedy like the Sicilian. There were sycophants and flatterers [1] also in the New Comedy, but they do not seem to have been sharply distinguished from the parasite. This parasite, whose position in the play is merely gastronomic, is one of the most absurd and lifeless of the whole cast. He serves, presumably, to introduce those passages concerning fish-sellers and cookery, which Athenaeus spent his life in collecting.[2] He is occasionally amusing, as in the *Epiclerus* of Diodorus, where he shows that Zeus was the first parasite, and that the profession gained position through the feasts in honour of Heracles. His good qualities he himself describes in the *Progonoi* of Antiphanes, where he says (fr. 195), ' You know my character. There is no nonsense about me. To my friends I am a friend. Touch me, I am like a rock. Shall I strike? I'm a thunderbolt. Shall I blind somebody? I am lightning. Bid me strangle any one you like, behold I am a noose. I am an earthquake to smash doors, a locust for jumping, a fly for feeding uninvited. I am like a well if you don't want some one to escape. Arrests, murders, testimonies, say the word, these are my game. So young men call me

---

[1] Antiph. 144; Anax. 49. The Κόλαξ of Menander, Struthias, was a parasite.

[2] Cf. the parasites in the *Curculio, Menaechmei,* etc.

Thunderbolt;[1] but I don't mind their jokes. Friend of my friends, I am a friend in deeds and not in words alone.'[2] Indeed, he is of service in the play in helping his patron to win his love, or in cheating the old man of money. Here he encroaches on the part of the slave, who doubles the parts attributed in tragedy to the *deus ex machina* and the chorus. It is doubtful whether a play ever existed without a slave, though the fact that he does not interest Athenaeus, except in numbers, excludes him from our fragments.[3] In the Roman translations, however, we see him at his best, since, as he is essentially non-Roman in character, he is unlikely to have lost or gained by the translation.

Of the other men characters, the most important are the cook and the soldier. Cooks must have played a considerable part in the subordinate scenes of the comedy, but, as they cannot have entered into the action of the domestic drama to any extent,[4] they will be considered later in the essay. The soldier of fortune, however, must have been continually on the stage. He is represented in Plautus and Terence as being the lover and the purchaser of the heroine, and therefore a being as much to be outwitted as are the fathers and the *lenones*. He was a mercenary, the only type of soldier known at Athens in the fourth century,

---

[1] σκηπτόν. This is obviously corrupt, but no better word has been suggested.

[2] The last lines are tragic from Euripides (Herwerden). Cf. Aristophon. 4. 10.

[3] Athen., vi. 81 *seq.*, quotes only Old Comedy. Our references to slaves are from Stobaeus. The importance of the slaves is shown in the prologue to the *Eunuch* of Terence, 35 *seq.* : 'Quod si personis isdem huic uti non licet : qui magis licet currentem servum scribere,' etc.

[4] Shadowy cooks are fairly important in the *Aulularia*.

a braggart and a bully. He tells endless stories about
his valour, which are as irrelevant as the catalogues of
food and dishes recited by the parasite and the cook.
Sometimes, indeed, he is an interesting and amusing
character, and when he is brutal and savage, he offers
an effective contrast to the elegance of the heroes and
the astuteness of the slaves and parasites.[1]

Of the women characters, the hetaira is as obviously
necessary to the plot as is her young lover, and when
she is old, as a ' *lena*,' she is equally important. Sometimes she seems to have been named after a prominent
courtesan of the time, conspicuously in the *Thais* of
Menander.[2] Of the free-born women, a recurrent type
is the mother of the hero, who has married a man
poorer than herself, and who entirely dominates him.
Then there is the daughter who has been seduced before
the action of the play, and whose seduction is her
important characteristic, not her personality.

These are the personages with whom we are acquainted
from the plays of Plautus and Terence. Besides them,
we know, from the titles, that there were others, which
seems to show a deeper knowledge of human nature,
and a greater variety in their delineation. Such are
the Ἄγροικος,[3] a man of complete insensibility and

---

[1] Especially in the *Miles Gloriosus* as a foil to Periplectomenus.
The soldier appears in the Στρατιώτης of Antiphanes, where he tells
a stupid tale of Cyprus (fr. 203), and in the Εἰσοικιζόμενος of Alexis,
etc. Menander's Thrasonides in the Μισούμενος, and Bias in the
Κόλαξ, Polemo in the Περικειρομένη, and Thrasyleon, were the most
notable examples.

[2] Martial, xiv. 187, Athen. xiii. p. 567, mentions the Φανίον ; and
Γλυκέρα perhaps was the subject of a play, if not the heroine in her
own name. Cf. Men. 569; Alciphro, *Ep.* ii. 4 ; cf. Meineke, *Men.
Phil. Rel.*, pp. 58, 73.

[3] Ἄγροικος was the name of plays by Anaxilas, Anaxandrides,

boorishness, the Ἀντερῶσα, the Ἀποκαρτερῶν,[1] the Αὑτοῦ ἐρῶν, the Δυσέρωτες, the Μισοπόνηρος,[2] the Παιδεραστής, the Φιλομήτωρ and Φιλοπάτωρ of Antiphanes; the Ἀντερῶν and Μαινόμενος of Anaxandrides; the Ἀσωτοδιδάσκαλος,[3] Εἰσοικιζόμενος, Δὶς πενθῶν, Μανδραγοριζομένη, Συναποθνῄσκοντες,[4] Συντρέχοντες, and others of Alexis; the Ἀνανεουμένη, Ἐξοικιζόμενος, Καταψευδόμενος, Ὑποβολιμαῖος, etc., of Philemon; the Ἄπληστος, Ἀπολιποῦσα, Ἑλλεβοριζόμενοι, Παιδερασταί, Πολυπράγμων of Diphilus; the Ἀνατιθεμένη, Δὶς ἐξαπατῶν,[5] Θεοφορουμένη, Μισογύνης, Μισούμενος, Ξενολόγος, Περικειρομένη,[6] Ῥαπιζομένη,[7] Ὑποβολιμαῖος, Ψοφοδέης of Menander, to quote only a few, and from the greatest poets. These were the characters whose introduction slightly varied the action of the plot. On the strength of some of them Guizot has imagined a New Comedy which, like Molière's, was more dependent on its psychology than its plot. But this question belongs to the critical

Philemon, and Menander. The meaning of the word is found in Aristotle, *Eth. Eud.* 1231 b, who quotes the use of it in the comic poets.

[1] Ἀποκαρτερῶν, besides, of Apollodorus Gelous and Philemon. It is the name of the book of Hegesias the Cyrenaic.—Ritt. and Preller, § 205 e.

[2] Of this play there is an illustrating fragment, but the space forbids quotation. The character enumerates the evils each of which is worse than the other (fr. 159).

[3] A fragment of this play on pleasure (25) will be given below.

[4] So Diphilus, translated by Plautus, *Commorientes*; Terence, *Prol. Adel.* 10.

[5] Probably the *Bacchides* of Plautus. Ritschl (cf. fr. 125, 126), *Parerg.* 407.

[6] For the Περικειρομένη, see Meineke, *Men. et Phil.* p. 136.

[7] The same place for the Ῥαπιζομένη; and Guizot, *Ménandre*, ch. v., for other characters.

part of the essay, and here it is enough to say that
the evidence of Plautus and Terence is against this
view, and that Pollux shows that the masks used only
pointed to certain types of character.[1]   There was
no room for a more delicate and sustained character-
drawing; these were only slightly different variations
of the usual types which are described above.

The characters, then, were conventional and expected;
to make them interesting it was necessary to invent a
continuous plot which would utilise the masks and
make them interesting.   The early Sicilian comedy
probably contained some kind of intrigue, and this
brings it nearer the New Comedy than the Old.   It
is possible, however, that since the time of Epicharmus
the two classes of play, topical and general, ran on
side by side.   This will explain the evolution of the
New Comedy better than any laws, which are, at best,
nebulous.   For when the chorus was dropped, the poets
would naturally be confined to the type of play which
dealt with life in general, and with the manners of
ordinary men rather than with those of Alcibiades.[2]

Yet it was probably the influence of tragedy which
determined the course of comedy.   Perhaps by parody-

---

[1] The characters are also to be found in Apuleius, *Flor.* 16, in which
passage the words *mediae comoediae scriptor* may be a gloss, since the
author states that Philemon *Fabulas cum Menandro in scaena dictavit,
certavitque cum eo*, unless Apuleius recognises a new comedy unknown
to us.

[2] It is not suggested that at the time of Aristophanes there was a
complete drama of intrigue.   This, though it is favoured by Aristotle
(*Poet.* 1449 b), who credits Crates with the first μῦθοι after Epicharmus
and Phormis, is unlikely.   But there may well have been a comedy
such as the one called Middle by the critics until recently.   An intrigue
of the New Comedy sort is not likely to have been used in comedy
before tragedy, though this, too, is possible.

ing the sister drama, comedy appropriated its conventions and sphere; perhaps the critical perception of the age saw the similarity between the two.[1] With the decline of tragedy came the growth of comedy, until the only difference between the two was that tragedy imitates men better than those we find in real life, comedy imitates those who are worse.[2]

In many ways we can see the influence of tragedy on comedy. It has been noticed above how tragedy in the fourth century declined from the ideals of the preceding generations. The characters were no longer individual and human, they had become typical and human. The conventions were improved, and stories were more freely varied from the original fables than in the preceding age. The rhetoric of the speakers was exaggerated. The chorus no longer made the moral reflections which are partly appropriate to the play, but, more generally, are obvious truths concerning all time and all people. We can see this in Euripides, and more so in his followers. This is obvious in the New Comedy, where the sententious utterances of the actors are sometimes paralleled by those of Euripides, sometimes his own words, sometimes more Euripidean than his own.[3] In the Old Comedy, it is doubtful whether a serious saying, with no sparkle of wit, would have been tolerated unless it were an obvious parody. But in the New Comedy we know to what an extent Euripides was admired for his style of aphorism if not

[1] At the end of the *Symposium*, Socrates makes Agathon and Aristophanes agree that tragedy and comedy ought to be written by the same man.

[2] Ar. *A. P.* 1448 a.

[3] For Euripidean lines in Menander see Meineke, *Epimetrum* ii., vol. iv., and Kock on the *Andria* of Menander.

for his general dramatic power, from the words of
Philemon, who says : 'If in truth the dead have senses,
as they say, I would hang myself, spectators, to see
Euripides.'

It is not in the style alone that Comedy was influ-
enced by tragedy. It is, generally, in the fact that
while one's interest in the Old Comedy was entirely
objective, in the New Tragedy and Comedy it was
subjective. Much as an Athenian might hate Cleon,
he would not have placed himself in the position of
the Sausage-Seller or of Demos, and in a fantasy like
the *Birds* he would have no particular interest in the
doings of any single character. But in the New
Tragedy the sympathy was for the hero of the piece.
His doings, his fortune, his downfall, were to be felt by
the whole theatre. That this is the case is shown by
the fact that some tragedians gave their plays a happy
ending to please the spectators.[1]   So in comedy the
audience followed the actions of the hero till virtue—or
its Greek equivalent—was rewarded, and vice and
avarice baffled. This places New Tragedy—where the
actions were less heroic—and New Comedy in a similar
position as regards the audience, while Old Comedy is
in direct opposition to either equally.

An examination of any play of Plautus or Terence
will show us how similar the structure of Comedy and
Tragedy had become. The plays begin with a prologue,[2] which was imitated directly from tragedy at

---

[1] Ar. *A.P.* 1452 b, *fin.* The 'ethical' interest of the greater tragedy
I have not introduced. It is obvious that it is as much opposed to
New Tragedy as to New Comedy. For the influence of Euripides on
Menander see Guizot, *Ménandre*, ch. viii., and cf. Quintilian, x. 1. 69.

[2] For the prologue, see Guizot, *op. c.* ch. iv.

quite an early period. It explains the antecedent events and prepares for the first Act; or it is introduced early in the first Act to explain what is coming. This was unnecessary in the best days of Tragedy, when the events to be recorded were well known, but it was used as soon as Tragedy began to depict events which were not the main part or the generally accepted version of a story. In the Comedy, which brings on the scene common people, it was necessary and was kept.

After the prologue comes the δέσις or piling up of the difficulties to introduce the crisis. This is as much tragic as comic, and should the περιπέτεια be arranged for the benefit of the old man, the play would be a tragedy—as we understand the word now. As it is, the plays of Plautus and Terence are nearly always inverted tragedies. For instance, in the *Phormio* of Terence, when Phanium is discovered to be the daughter of Chremes, the change of fortune is good for the young man, but nothing less than a tragedy for Chremes, who wishes to keep his former marriage unknown. So, too, in the *Asinaria* of Plautus, the play ends unhappily for the father, though his by no means virtuous conduct on the stage may be the excuse for this. But in the *Phormio*, since the misdeeds of Chremes are earlier than the action of the story, the retribution is as tragic as in any baser tragedy. However, since all comedy of this class, when one man's good fortune means bad fortune to another, is so near to tragedy, we must not lay too much stress on this point. The real influence of tragedy is in the general character of the plays; the similarity of the interest excited, of construction, of language and idea.

c

When tragedy and comedy both produced plays identical in form, it is impossible to deny that tragedy had its influence on comedy, and, further, since it was Euripides who lowered tragedy to its fourth-century level, it must be acknowledged that he was the initiator of the comedy which sprang from his tragedies. And we find in the double plays of Euripides, the *Alcestis* and *Orestes*, the identical construction of the many double comedies of Plautus and Terence, in which the son, or sons, attain their desire, the fathers are satisfied, and all ends happily.

The exact character of the plays of the New Comedy can never be realised until the possible manuscript of Menander is discovered. The evidence we have is of two kinds: that of the Roman translations, and that of the fragments and titles. For the intrigue and plots of the plays, we must rely entirely on the first, and for the characters, we can use both, for, to a great extent, one agrees with the other. But, alone, the Roman translations are untrustworthy. Terence, though he boasts that he keeps nearer the Greek than the others, himself acknowledges that he adapted scenes from one play to another. By doing this, he secures, of course, a greater variety of incident than did the original authors, and probably reaches a greater confusion of the unities. His characters, however, are more Greek than those of Plautus, whose personages, though fundamentally Hellenic, always seem to be acting in accordance with the proverb, and trying to do in Rome as the Romans did. It was understood when these plays were acted that the scene was in Greece. The Romans spoke of themselves as *Barbari*, but, to balance this, the characters constantly explain that they are acting in a Greek way—*congraecari*,[1] *pergraecari*. Frequently the Plautine characters speak as Romans, quite apart from their nature as Greeks on the stage. Therefore, while Terence by 'contamination' hides the original, Plautus does so by an adaptation of plays, which is not translation.

Yet the Roman translations are more valuable—especially as their evidence is corroborated by what we know from commentators about the New Comedy—in judging the intrigue power of the New Comedy, than are the fragments. These come from two sources only, and just those sources which preserve the least necessary and informing. But they are exceedingly useful in showing us some of the characters often used, and the style of the dialogue and monologue.

Athenaeus, a learned Alexandrian, collected passages concerning food and the general manners of the table from all the plays he knew. These are in the main valueless, and have caused some to think that the Middle Comedy, at least, was devoted to praise of the delights of eating. This is, of course, unfounded, for Athenaeus has preserved most of the extant fragments of Aristophanes and the Old Comedy, while the plays show us that eating is a very unimportant part of the Comedy. Often the addresses to articles of diet contained a parody, as in the *Acharnians* a parody of the *Alcestis* is found in Dicaeopolis' address to the eel.[2] Plautus shows us that others of these cookery fragments were spoken by the parasites, and the

---

[1] This may be paralleled by the use of the word ἑλληνικῶς in Antiph. fr. 184. Cf. Sellar, *Roman Poets of the Republic*, p. 167 *seq.*

[2] Ar. *Ach.* 891-894. Cf. Address to an eel, Eub. 35, and other tragic passages; Antiphanes 105, etc.

metres[1] in which these catalogues of dishes are written,
show that they are the *cantica* introduced to gag a
pause in the action of the play.

Again, the passages concerning fishmongers and
cooks, so constantly recurring among the fragments,
are the spoils of Athenaeus. They show that the
Comedy ridiculed fishmongers and cooks, but not that
they were its chief stock-in-trade. Had there been
a curious jurist or antiquary who collected references
to the trades in the minor paths of Greek literature,
we should have had an equally complete picture of
some other sides of the characters.

Our other source of fragments is Stobaeus, who
collected, for the good of his son, hundreds of fatiguing
moral reflections on old age, women, life, and kindred
subjects, in a way that proves him a man lamentably
wanting in humour. These fragments, however, are
valuable, for they show the manner and matter of
the speeches, just as Athenaeus shows us some of the
favourite types of the Comedy. Both help us in
testing the evidence of the Roman writers as regards
style and character-drawing, but in regard to the plots
we are almost dependent on Plautus and Terence.

We have, however, many testimonies to the importance of the plot. The earliest is an extant fragment
of Antiphanes, who was considered the typical poet of
the plotless Middle Comedy. 'To write tragedy,' he
says in the Ποίησις, 'To write tragedy is easy in every
way. For the audience knows the stories before a word

---

[1] The most conspicuous passages are the description of the feasts at
the marriage of Iphicrates (Anaxandr. 41), and a fragment of Mnesimachus, which contain seventy-one and sixty-five anapaestic lines
respectively.

is uttered, and the poet need only remind them. If
Oedipus be mentioned, they know all that is coming,
his father Laius, his mother Iocast, his daughters, his
sons, his sufferings, his fate. And if Alcmeon is named,
every child can tell at once that he killed his mother in
a fit of anger, and that Adrastus will come on the stage
in anger, and then go off. . . . Again, when they can
say no more, and their invention has failed them,
they lift up the gods on the machine, as easily as
one lifts one's finger, and this satisfies the audience.
But this is not our luck. We must invent everything,
names, former deeds, present actions, *dénouement*, en-
tries. Should Chremes or Pheido fail in any one of
these conditions, he is hissed off the stage. The liberty
of doing anything is only allowed to Peleus and Teucer.'[1]

In the plays of this poet we find a few traces, besides the titles, of the commonplace intrigue of the
New Comedy. In the *Neottis*, which was probably
played about Ol. 109. 2, and which is named after a
hetaira, we have a few lines from the speech of a boy
who came to Athens with his sister as a slave. Some
of the moral sayings prove almost conclusively that the
young-man-and-courtesan play was popular in his day,
such for instance as that on bad luck in the 'Ηνίοχος,
that on a citizen hetaira in the 'Υδρία, and several of
the unattached fragments.[2]

But it was in the time of Menander that intrigue
had become the most important part of the play. It
is said[3] that he considered the plot as everything, the
writing as of no difficulty. The character-drawing is

---

[1] Antiph. fr. 191.
[2] *Ibid.* frr. 104, 168, 212, 263, 261, 262, etc.
[3] Plutarch, *Bellone an Pace praest. Athen.* iv.

not mentioned. This is in accordance with the *Poetics* of Aristotle, whose precepts Menander clearly followed.[1] But it is not to be imagined that Menander and the other poets invented really new intrigues. From the Roman translations, and the notes of Donatus and other commentators, we know the character of these plays. They are astonishingly similar. The only difference is in the introduction of some new variation of character or incident. As a rule, the basis of the plot is of one of three kinds.

The παρθένων φθοραί were the subjects of many of these plays. A good example is found in the *Aulularia* of Plautus. Here the φθορά is antecedent to the action of the play, as it nearly always was, and is explained in the prologue. The turn of fortune is brought on by a recognition of some ring or charm which the hero gave the maiden, or, as in the *Hecyra*, stole from her. By a necessary convention the man is never seen by the girl whom he violates, nor knows who she is. Of one of these plays by Menander, the Πλόκιον, and of its Roman translation by Caecilius, we have several fragments. The plot is briefly this: Simon has a rich wife and a son. Menedemus is poor and has a daughter. The two fathers are friends, and Simon's son has violated the daughter of Menedemus, of course not knowing who she was. The ἀναγνώρισις must have taken place by means of the πλόκιον, and the remainder of the play would be given to the reconciliation of Crobyla, the rich wife, to her son's marriage.[2] The poverty of

---

[1] Ar. *A.P.*, ch. viii. ix., etc. ; Guizot, *Ménandre*, ch. iv.

[2] This Πλόκιον has more points of resemblance than the names with the *Heautontimoroumenos* of Terence. Παρθένων φθοραί, besides the *Aulularia*, are the *Adelphi*, *Hecyra* of Terence, the Φάσμα of Menander

this plot was of course hidden by the scenes where Crobyla and Simon quarrel, and by the birth of the heroine's daughter. This latter scene is a favourite with both Plautus and Terence, and certainly was found in Menander.[1]

Akin to these plays are those where the ἑταῖραι are proved to be citizens, but whether they can be considered παρθένων φθοραί depends on whether a free woman is a free woman till she is proved to be one. This is the comic counterpart of the tragedies of *Oedipus* and *Merope*;[2] the recognition is the cause of the good fortune to both hero and heroine. These were perhaps the most frequent of all the plays. Generally, a young man is enamoured of some hetaira, and has not enough money to buy her. Her owner is on the point of selling her to some other man—a soldier by preference—when the slave gets the money, by some wiles, from the hero's father, and is just going to purchase her for his master when she is found to be a citizen. In some cases the slave's tricks are found out, and all would be upset if the ἀναγνώρισις did not occur. This is a double plot, like the ones mentioned above. Each play differed from the other by some change in the manner and cause of the recognition.[3]

The other plots are those where the object of the hero is to purchase a hetaira who does not prove to be a citizen. In these the variety is obtained through

(Donatus, *Pro. Eun.* 9), where the ἔρωτες are certain and the φθορά probable, but not necessary.

[1] Terence, *Andria, Adelphi*; Plautus, *Aulularia*; Menander, Ἀνδρία, frr. 40, 41.

[2] Ar. *Eth. Nic.* iii. ch. i. Ignorance πρὸς τί or περὶ τί.

[3] Examples of this kind are many: *Poenulus, Curculio, Rudens, Cistellaria, Phormio, Andria*.

the different ways by which the slaves or the hero get money. There is probably an example in the *Thesaurus* of Menander. Here, we know from Donatus,[1] the hero was a young man whose father had left a treasure in his grave. An old man bought the tomb, and the play turns on a lawsuit between the young man and the owner. The monument we may believe to have been sold to pay for some love-affair, and the treasure was probably required for the same purpose. These plays are common in Plautus, the most prominent being the *Mostellaria*.[2]

The essential feature of the New Comedy then is the intrigue. A new scene, a new trick of the slave, a slight change in the ordinary character of the old man, were the distinctive marks of each play. In those days it was never necessary to produce anything quite original. Poets borrowed from one another, as the recurrent titles and fragments show; it is said that Menander took his Δεισιδαίμων completely from the Οἰωνιστής of Antiphanes.[3] Whether this is true or not, it is natural that plagiarism was no sin. We must remember the conditions for which a play was written. An author produced one play for each yearly festival; it was heard and then forgotten. Even if they were

---

[1] Donatus, Prologue Ter. *Eunuch*, 10. Cf. *Trinummus* of Plautus.

[2] There were of course other plays, like the *Menaechmei* and the *Amphitruo*, where the intrigue is complicated by the 'Comedy of Errors' motive. But even in these the hetaira is by no means absent from the interest of the play. The *Captivi* is an experiment in the 'Recognition' series.

[3] Caecilius *ap. Porphyr. Euseb. Praep. Evang.* 2, p. 273, and compare Terence, prol. to *Andria*: 'Menander fecit Andriam et Perinthiam, qui utramvis recte novit, ambas noverit; non ita dissimili sunt argumento, at tamen dissimili oratione sunt factae et stilo.'

read, the case is the same. In an age of criticism and
not creation it was the cleverness of contrivance, not
the material of the play, that was admired; consequently the rearrangement of old matter was almost
as acceptable as the invention of new.

IV.—OTHER PLAYS

I have now dealt with that class of comedy which is
considered most characteristic of the New Comedy. In
the next place, it is necessary to examine such plays of
the fourth century as do not appear from their titles
and fragments to have been merely domestic. These
plays, as I have noted above, are found in the greatest
frequency in the earlier poets, such as Antiphanes,
Eubulus, Anaxandrides, and Alexis; less often in
Philemon and Diphilus, and but rarely in Menander.
Of the post-Menandrian dramatists so few titles and
fragments are preserved that they must almost be left
out of the question.

It should be noticed before discussing these plays
that the length of the comedies had probably decreased
greatly when the Chorus was finally dropped. We
know that, instead of three, as in the fifth century,
five plays were produced annually at the two festivals,
and it is possible that many of the plays were written
to be read and not acted, and that others were acted
outside Athens. But even with this allowance, it is
probable that comedies were shorter. Everything lends
itself to this theory. The slender threads of interest
in most of the plays could only be protracted by the
introduction of topical and episodic scenes, after the
fashion of Aristophanes. That this was not the case

we learn from Aristotle, where he points to the episodic as the worse form of play, and from the anonymous writer who defines the (Middle and) New Comedy as principally concerned with plots, and from the habit of Terence of knitting two plays of Menander into one.[1]

Most prominent of all the plays, which were not domestic, were the parodies. Of these we have few traces, considering them as different from the ordinary ridicule of Mythological Characters. They were, more probably, the subjects used by the real Middle Comedy (403-388), when they were either burlesques of the poets and of their styles, or caricatures of great men. In the New Comedy there was much parody of the words of the poets, especially of their periphrasis, but the burlesque of the stories used was very nearly the same as the ordinary fabulous comedy. The cause of this is simple, and is explained above as the natural result of the tendency of the tragedians to reduce their heroes to an ignoble level, and to introduce other persons who are not 'imitations of superior men.' If Euripides is guilty of this he is also guilty of a parody of his predecessor. For in the *Electra* he ridicules the rather clumsy recognition of Aeschylus, and is, therefore, imitating comedy, or introducing a phase of it.

Of direct parody of the tragedians, we have few signs except the titles.[2] Of their style there are frequent ridiculous imitations, nearly all of them consisting of

---

[1] An instance of expansion in Plautus is evident in the *Miles Gloriosus*. A whole scene (iii. 1) is given up to the moral reflections of Periplectomenus which are collected from several sources.

[2] The *Aeolus* of Antiphanes contains one quite serious fragment, and another which is characteristically comic (18, 19).

periphrases of food. Thus, in Antiphanes, there is a
dialogue (fr. 1) in which a character utters an encomium,
which it is impossible to translate, on barley-cake and
stuffed kid. 'What is that you are saying?' says the
other character. 'I am finishing a tragedy of Sophocles.' In another passage (fr. 52) of the same poet,
one man says, 'When I wish to speak of a pot to you,
do I call it a pot? or do I say, Vessel shaped by the
turning of the wheel, hollow-bodied, moulded of clay,
and roasted in another chamber of the mother; holding
tender-fleshed, milk-fed forms of the new-born flock
baked in itself?' 'By Heracles,' says the other, 'you
will kill me if you don't say, straight out, Stew-pot.'
But this sort of thing continues in this fragment, and is
found in many more.

Another poet ridicules the sigmatism of Euripides,[1]
and Axionicus in his Φιλευριπίδης has a parody on a
choral ode.

We have no traces of a play which parodied the
recognitions and gods from machines, though they probably were burlesqued. Most of the fragments suggest
those fabulous stories which are merely representations
of heroes as ordinary men, and are therefore on the
borders of domestic drama. The favourite character
of course was Heracles, who, in several plays called
Βούσιρις, Ὀμφάλη, etc., was a gluttonous Theban.
In the Linus of Alexis, Heracles is given the choice
of several books, Homer, Hesiod, Tragedies, Epicharmus, and finally chooses one on cookery.[2] Perhaps
this is the play where Linus is represented as having
three pupils, of whom Heracles was the slowest to learn
music. When his master rebuked him, he broke his

---

[1] Eubulus 26, 27.   [2] Alexis 135.

cithara on Linus' head.[1]   In the *Busiris* of Ephippus, the hero fights like an Argive,[2] getting drunk before the combat and always running away.

From the *Ganymede* of Antiphanes we have a considerable fragment.[3]   Laomedon asks the pedagogue what he knows of the rape of the boy.   'Is that a riddle you are asking me?   Do you know anything about the rape of the boy? or has it some real meaning?' says the pedagogue.   'Slaves,' cries the king, 'give me a strap and quickly.'   'Well, I give it up,' answers the pedagogue, 'but are you going to punish me?   That's not correct.   I ought to drink a cup of salt water.'   In the *Asclepius* of the same writer, some one complains of a doctor, probably the god himself, who deceived an old Bruttian slave by giving her some quack mixture.[4]   In the Σαπφώ the poetess is a riddle-propounder, and her loves with Archilochus and Hipponax were the subject of a play by Diphilus.[5]

Contemporary allusions, of course, were common in these plays.   In the *Heracles* of Anaxandrides, which was probably about Linus, there is a fragment on musicians in which Argas is named.   In the *Theseus* of the same author there is a reference to Plato.   Some of these burlesques would seem to be satires on the manners of different cities.   The legend of Odysseus would easily be used for this purpose.   Thus in the *Odysseus* of Anaxandrides there is a fragment on the slang of Athens, and one on the fish-sellers.   In the *Antiope* of Eubulus, Zethos is commanded to go to the 'holy plain of Thebes,' and to live there, because loaves

---

[1] Diod. 3. 67.   [2] Ephippus 2; cf. 17.
[3] Antiph. 74.   [4] Antiph. 425; Philetairos 1.
          [5] Diphilus 69; Athen. 13. 599 d.

are cheap in that city, while Amphion goes to Athens.
The latter is evidently curious about Callistratus, and
to the former some Boeotian describes his race, in the
formula sanctioned by comic usage, as πώνειν καὶ φαγεῖν
μέγ' ἀνδρικοί. In another play,[1] some one is beginning
to describe the procedure at a sacrifice, when, unfor-
tunately, he breaks off. In the Κέρκωπες of Eubulus
there are two fragments, presumably from the speech
of Heracles, in which he describes Corinth and Thebes.

With the nature of these mythological comedies we
are familiar through the *Amphitruo* of Plautus. In
that play Jupiter is another Amphitruo, and Mercury
is Sosia, the son of Davos. The humour of the play is
in the confusion of Amphitruo and the libertinage of
Jupiter; the story scarcely deserves the name of plot.
Jupiter is but a love-lorn old man, dominated by Juno,
as Demaenetus, of the *Asinaria*, is by his wife, Arte-
mona. The divine power of assuming the form of a
man creates a story like that of the twins in the
Menaechmei.[2] So, probably, in the other plays it is an
almost domestic incident[3] which introduces the characters of mythology, and there is added to the interest
of the plot that pleasure which is felt from the representation of superior beings as our equals. This is
noticed by Dio Chrysostom,[4] who says that in comedy
a drunken Cario or Dio does not cause a laugh, but
Heracles in that state is funny, especially if he be

---

[1] The *Odysseus* of Eubulus (fr. 71), called also Πανόπται.

[2] There is a line in the ῞Υμνις of Menander which suggests a similar
plot (fr. 474): Νῦν δὲ κατὰ πόλιν | εὕρηκε τὸν ἕτερον, τὸν σέ, τὸν ἐμὲ
τουτονί.

[3] Cf. the plots mentioned in frr. 47 and 48 of Amphis.

[4] 32, p. 699 R.

brought on the stage wearing a yellow robe, as the slaves are usually represented. It was not in comedy alone that the Greeks were irreverent. Heracles is a drunken boor in the *Alcestis*, and probably the Satyric plays gave the hint to the comic writers. On vases, too, we see moments in the life of the heroes which are by no means conceived in the spirit of reverence.

If the mythological plays were comic stories of the lives of the gods and heroes, the plays named after dead men and foreigners were probably similar. Some of them, however, were named after men, living or dead, characteristic of a certain class, and would contain a satire on that class, or a story dealing with them. These, like the *Plato* of Aristophon, and the *Nereus* of Anaxilas and Anaxandrides, will be discussed later. The others are named after famous men who are dead, or after foreigners. These cannot be considered deliberate instances of κωμῳδεῖν ὀνομαστί, nor can those which are named after citizens.[1] For, if they were, it is difficult to see in what respects they would differ from the Old Comedy; and, even if the laws are all apocryphal, it is evident that had this kind of play been popular, it would have been more common, and if it were unpopular enough to have died at the beginning of the century, it seems impossible that an occasional instance could be found even at the end of the century. The plays on dead men would be merely a picture of some person like the titular hero in character. Such are the *Theramenes*,[2] who might have

---

[1] It is difficult to know in the fourth century who were citizens and who were ξένοι. A list of possible individual plays will be found in Meineke, i. pp. 274, 438.

[2] Cratinus the younger. The *Euripus* is a play of Philemon.

been called Εὔριπος, the *Lampo*[1] which merely meant Οἰωνιστής, the *Leonidas*,[2] who probably was a Thrasyleon, and the *Cleobulina*. In the case of the foreigners, if Zeus and the other gods could be used to give dignity to the ordinary domestic play, surely a foreigner of lascivious habits would do as well. In that case the remarks about the persons would be no more objectionable than those incidental allusions which we find scattered over the comedy of the whole age.

Most of these remarks are absurd references to living people as big eaters or big drinkers. Callimedon[3] the orator is continually being mentioned as a fish-eater or something of the sort. So, too, are Mato, Euthynos, Phocricides,[4] and several others. The luxurious life of the tyrants is continually being mentioned. Alexander is twice named by Menander, once as a big drinker, and the other time as a swift traveller.[5] Philip is referred to by Antiphanes, in rather an obscure way, as one who did not pay his club subscription.[6] Demosthenes[7] is laughed at for his catch saying, δοῦναι καὶ ἀποδοῦναι, and for his invocation, μὰ γῆν, μὰ κρήνας, μὰ ποταμούς, μὰ νάματα. He is mentioned with the other orators in the Δῆλος (Δήλιος) of Timocles in a fragment which is worth translating :—

'A. Demosthenes has got 50 talents.

B. Lucky man! provided he does not give any away.

A. And Mocrocles has received a lot of gold.

---

[1] A play of Antiphanes. [2] *Ibid.*

[3] Καλλιμέδων, called Κάραβος, Antiph. 26. 76, Alexis 193. 56, Eubulus 9, and in several other places.

[4] Perhaps a play of Strato's called after him.

[5] Men. 293, 924 ; cf. *Adesp.* 299, 300, 301. [6] Antiph. 124.

[7] (i) Antiph. 169. (ii) 296. ; Timocles 38. (iii) *Id.* 4, and there is a fragment, *id.* 10, which perhaps refers to him, *q.v.* and *Adesp.* 294.

B. The giver is a fool, the recipient is in luck.

A. Demon and Callisthenes received some too.

B. They were poor, so I excuse them.

A. The clever-tongued Hyperides was given some.

B. He will make the fish-sellers rich; he is so fond of fish that by comparison sharks seem Syrians.'

There was, however, more violent abuse against Demochares in a play of Archedicus.[1] He is accused of the worst crimes in a way that it is doubtful whether the Old Comedy could parallel. So, too, Philippides characterises Demetrius with Aristophanic exaggeration as 'He who cut down the year to one month, he who treated the Acropolis as an inn and brought hetairae up to Athene herself; he through whom the frost destroyed the vines, through whose impiety the holy robe was torn in half, he who reduced the honours of the gods to what is due to a mortal,—it is he who harms the city, not the comedy.'

As a general rule, however, this badinage is innocent enough. It belonged to the πομπεία, which was allowed at the Dionysia and festivals. Nothing can be decided by the help of these fragments as to the nature of the plays. We can only say that the poets could bring in more or less irrelevant libel as well as irrelevant morality.[2]

Some of these plays seem to have dealt with particular peoples or classes. The titles are frequent enough, and tell us very little. But, from the evidence of Plautus and Terence, we know that these plays were not, to any great extent, concerned with people of the nation or

---

[1] Polybius xiii. 13; cf. *Adesp.* 303, 312.

[2] Theon. *Soph. prog.* iv. 199, Walz.: ὁ γὰρ τελευταῖος στίχος ἐκ περιττοῦ πρόσκειται θηρώμενος μόνον τὸν παρὰ τῶν θεατῶν ἔπαινον (*de* Men. fr. 354).

employment denoted in the title. The *Poenulus*, the *Mercator*, the *Persa*, the *Andria*, are all plays of the ordinary domestic type, and so, too, we may conjecture, were the frequent Ἐπιδαύριος, Βοιωτίς, Κορινθία, Βαβυλώνιος, Κιθαριστής, Ἰατρός, Ζωγράφος, Φιλαθηναῖος, Φιλοθηβαῖος, and others of the New Comedy. Of course each of these plays contained one character that was not quite the same, in nationality or profession, as those in every other play, just in the same way as those plays mentioned above contained one character of slightly differing nature.

Just as with men, we have frequent allusions to particular peoples. Athens herself was not untouched, and, as I have noted above, may have been the object of satire in some Mythological comedies. In two fragments[1] Athens is mentioned for its excellence in certain productions, chiefly figs and water. In this I see a reference to the sycophants and law-courts. In the Πόλεις of Anaxandrides there is a dialogue between an Egyptian[2] and an Athenian.

Plato and the philosophers are continually being ridiculed, not only in side passages, but also with full prominence. They, as well as the characters mentioned above, and the cooks, must, of course, have entered into the plots of the domestic plays. But it is natural that in the earlier days of comedy they were afforded greater prominence, and that they were more important when the plot was not yet fully developed. Yet the fact that they appear so often among the fragments does

---

[1] Antiph. 177, Eubulus 74. Cf. the numerous fragments which give lists of eatables and whence they come, *e.g.* Ant. 193, 236, Eub. 19 and c.

[2] Anax. 39; cf. Timocles 1, Antiph. 147. For the play cf. Heniochus 5.

not show that they were continually on the scene or mentioned by the speakers. Just as the fishmongers and cooks owe their importance to Athenaeus, so the passages about Plato were collected by Diogenes Laertius,[1] and the ones mentioning the food of the Pythagoreans by the 'learned pig.' It is really surprising that we have not more passages about them, for Diogenes has collected such trivial remarks that it seems as if he collected all he could. Of the plays named after philosophers we have the Φιλόσοφοι of Philemon, the *Plato* of Aristophon, the *Pythagorist* of the same author, the Πυθαγορίζουσα of Alexis and Cratinus junior,[2] of none of which we have a vestige of a plot. There is, however, some likelihood that the story about Lacydes, in Numenius, is from a late comic play.[3] In it, Lacydes locks his store-chest, seals it up and throws the seal into the box through a hole in the lid. His slaves find out the trick, and open the box; whereat the master is much surprised, and repairs to the philosophers to learn about 'disappearances.' This might be merely a comedy to ridicule the philosophers, but it is more probable that the store-chest was a treasure-box, and that this was the plan by which the slaves stole the father's money to pay for the amours of his son. It would then be only another variation on the usual theme, 'Given a boy in love, to find the money he requires.' The store-chest seems rather curious, and it is only natural that the holy father would ignore the worldly side of the play.

From the fragments we can reconstruct little. There

---

[1] Diog. Laer. 3. 22.

[2] Perhaps also the Ταραντῖνοι of the same two authors.

[3] Numen. *Euseb. Praep. Evang.* 14. 7; Hirzel, *Hermes* xviii. 389.

are references to the food of the Pythagoreans in many places, and a reason given for their abstinence in the *Pythagorist* of Aristophon.[1] Plato and his disciples are described as looking into the nature of a cucumber.[2] Plato is referred to as one who knows everything,[3] and as one who can only frown, and make his eyebrows spiral like a shell.[4] His theory on love and the good are mentioned,[5] as are his luxury and pretty habits,[6] and his liking for olives.[7] Menander[8] says that Crates gave his daughter to one of his disciples ' on approval ' for thirty days, and Epicurus is mentioned by Hegesippus and Bato.[9] Similarly those who are given over to the rites of Cybele are ridiculed by Menander in the Ἱέρεια.[10] But these references are all in the third person, and are merely introduced to give local colour to the plays. The only instance where anything approaching ridicule—not mere mention—of a philosophy is introduced, as far as I can remember, is in a curious passage of Antiphanes, where the arguments of the Eleatics are jumbled together to form a nonsense passage.[11]

---

[1] Aristophon 9 ; cf. Antiph. 134, 135, 160, 188, 226, 227 ; Aristophon 12, 13 ; Alexis 27, 220, 221 ; Mnesimachus 1 ; *Adesp.* 275.

[2] Epicrates 11.   [3] Alexis 1.   [4] Amphis 13.

[5] *Id.* 6, 15 ; Alexis 152 ; Philippides 6.

[6] Antiph. 33, of one of his school ; Ephipp. 14.

[7] Anaxandrides 19. Other references to Plato are Cratinus jun. 10, Ophelio 3, Alexis 147, 158, 180.

[8] Men. 117, 118.

[9] Hegisippus 3 ; Bato 3, 5. Aristippus is mentioned, Alexis 36 ; Zeno, Philemon 85 ; Crates, *id.* 146 ; Men. 117, 118 ; *Adesp.* 120. A man who may be Heracleides Ponticus, Antiph. 113. The law of Demetrius Phalereus against Philosophers, Alexis 94. Democritus and Epicurus in a speech of a cook, Damoxenos 2 ; Xenocrates, *Adesp.* 292.

[10] Men. 202, 245, 326.   [11] Antiph. 122.

Of the other classes which were ridiculed, and which may have occasioned plays consisting in this ridicule alone, the most important is that of the fish-sellers. We have numerous fragments concerning them, which, like those containing cookery lists, probably came from the mouths of slaves and parasites. Nearly all are descriptive, and only one seems to belongs to a scene which may have contained a fish-stall. It is in the Ἁλιευομένη of Antiphanes (fr. 26), and the sale of fish is acutely mingled with personalities. There is not a single play named Ἰχθυοπώλης, which is astonishing if the fish-sellers really did appear on the scene.

In the later authors the place of importance in the fragments is given to the cook. Unlike the fish-sellers, he has plays named after him, and many of the fragments are his own words. This is natural, for he could easily be introduced into the domestic plays, since he was a public caterer going from house to house in the exercise of his art. Therefore he was a well-known and important character in Athens, and the representation of him as an artist, a philosopher, an atomist, a general, or a Homeric scholar, is certainly comic.[1] It is even probable that he was founded on fact, for, of all the minor artists, even in our own day, we are told the cook considers himself the most important.

The parasites have been described above; it is only necessary here to mention that some of them are men-

---

[1] Cooks in Athenaeus ix. 20-24, 68-70; vii. 32, 36-41. Cf. Menander, 462, 518, 130, 'No one wrongs a cook with impunity, ours is a sacred art'; Anaxippus 1; Hegesippus 1; Sosipater 1; Euphron 1. 10. 11; Macho 2, 'the music of cookery'; Bato 4, 'the studious cook'; Posidonius 26; and innumerable others. The many references to τέχνη collected by Stobaeus probably are from the cooks.

tioned by name, notably Tithymallus and Chaerephon.
One more class, however, is conspicuous. The Hetairae
belong more properly to the entirely domestic plays,
where they were mentioned, but the fact that many
of them gave name to plays has led historians to believe
that these plays were written to ridicule them alone.
This is, of course, possible, just as it is possible in
regard to the plays named after philosophers,—which
are few, and to those named after fishmongers,—which
do not exist at all. There are plays named after
hetairae in the works of nearly every poet of whom
we have any considerable fragments. There are remarks
made upon individuals, and strictures passed on the
whole class. None of these are distinctive of any
class of play other than the domestic. For it is only
natural that, in the earlier comedy, the old man or
the slave, when recounting the miseries of a debauched
life, should mention names, and even give a detailed
picture, like the one where several notorious hetairae
are likened to monsters,[1] or the one where their
wiles are shown.[2] Even the famous Ἀντίλαις of
Epicrates need not have been a tirade against the
courtesan Lais. For, in Ἀντιλέων and Ἀντίθεος, I
find good authority for translating the word 'Peer
of Lais,' and thus reducing it to a fanciful name for
a fictitious hetaira.

V.—CRITICAL

It is natural that the New Comedy, which was concerned with a superficial view of mankind, should not
produce characters either extraordinary in their indivi-

---

[1] Anaxilas 22.　　　　[2] Alexis 98.

duality like those of the Old Comedy, nor ordinary like those of the present day. It was neither idealist nor realist. For by idealistic one understands those characters which embody some great virtue or principle, and by realistic, those which, by their thorough likeness of the objects imitated, are convincing and true. Realism does not deal with classes, but only with individuals, and it is evident that the characters of the New Comedy are never individuals, but types. But the types of the New Comedy are not drawn as are the ideal characters of tragedy. For while the old tragedians created characters by making their individuality stronger than life through the gift of certain virtues, the New Comedy made a collection of superficial qualities, and endowed them with bodies. Nor is it only in tragedy that these ideal characters have their place. We can see in modern comedy those personages who are greater than men because they have greater virtues, and yet are greater than men though they have greater faults. It is not because the distortion of a bad quality makes men lower than they are, while the development of virtues makes them greater. For it is obvious that such characters as are made of a mere collection of good qualities are no more artistic than those made of bad. A soldier typical of the braver, more modest class, is no more true or interesting than one who is typically a coward and a braggart. The great distinction between the artistic creations of great men and critical caricatures of certain qualities lies in the fact that the former act as men, the latter as masks.

In contradistinction with the realistic imitations of our day these characters of the New Comedy appear

ideal. For ideal has two meanings : one as applied to
certain universal virtues and vices of the human mind,
and the other to particular and, more or less, external
qualities. It is the distinction between the εἶδος of
good and bad, and the εἶδος of a tinker or a tailor.
Of the first an idealised embodiment would contain
more good than an ordinary man, of the second more
tinkerishness than an ordinary tinker. This second
idealism is clearly opposed to realism. In real life
men participate to a certain extent in the general
characteristics of their class, they are never the class
itself to those who look into their characters. Again,
men have reasons, external and internal, for adopting
the habits of, and for acting in accordance with, this
distinctive quality. And it is this which brings the
great Tragedy of the fifth century nearer to realism
than the New Comedy. When Sophocles drew an
Antigone, he showed, in the play itself, the environ-
ment and the mental process which determined the
expression of her characteristic virtue. She is ideal
in her nature, she is human in the workings of her
nature.

Similarly Molière in his *Tartuffe* has so drawn his
character that the whole play depends on him, and the
intrigue illustrates, as it revolves round, him. But in
the New Comedy, as a general rule, it is postulated by
the conventional masks of the personages that they
represent certain types. They go through the plays
as one of their number might act in real life, but we
do not see their characters in any new light, nor have
we any reason for their acting except the fact that it
is the way of parasites, and that the mask denotes
a parasite. There seems a complete absence of those

touches which tell us what is occurring in the brain of the actor. This is evident from a comparison of the old men in the *Phormio*, and in the *Fourberies de Scapin*. In Terence, we know from the mask of the old man that he is angry; in Molière's play the half-comic, half-sad, ' Que diable alloit-il faire dans cette galère ? ' shows us more of the internal tumult of the tricked Géronte than does all Terence's conventional storming and swearing. It was enough for the spectators that the old man should be tricked; they had no interest in the old man himself.

When a particularly well defined character is introduced, he is in the background, or is a subordinate character of the play. The Euclio of the *Aulularia* is the strongest character of the Roman dramatists and comes nearest to the ideal. But it has been said of him, that not he, but his pot of gold, is the essential character of the play. This is not true entirely, for his character gives light and position to an otherwise ordinary play. But it is true that it is not he who influences the intrigue, but his gold, and this becomes evident when the play is compared with the *Avare*. The Menedemus of Terence acts in accordance with the epithet given him by the title only at the beginning of the play, and the *Truculentus* might be any other slave.

It is, then, with typical characters, with the internal and external masks which show them to belong to a certain class, that the play deals. Again and again they appeared on the scene, in parts to which they were accustomed, to fill a place which was made for them to fill. It is, as it were, a comedy of chessmen, each piece performing its own moves with a tiresome consistency. It would be unnecessary to criticise the psychology of the New Comedy by the standard of truth. No man, as I have said, is a type; each man, for artistic purposes, is an individual. But in drawing these characters, the poets were only guilty of a fault which was common in the Greek mind at the time. The creative mood had given way to the critical, and a passion had arisen for arguing from the particular to the general in everything. In psychology points of resemblance were collected in individuals to construct from them types. From Aristotle we find that the people had a tendency to group characters in the two extremes of each quality, leaving the middle unnamed and unallotted. Whether Aristotle and Theophrastus borrowed their characters from Comedy or lent them to it is an irrelevant question. The fact that these distinctions, broad and labelled, are to be found in both, shows that it was considered satisfactory by the Athenians of the day.

It was a complete absence of poetry that caused the writers of the New Comedy to adopt these characters. They were not creators, and consequently could not imagine great characters; they were critics, and therefore they drew men as they saw them through the eyes of their time and people. It requires a fresh and young and vigorous age to create; the New Comedy is the voice of a decadent people. It is quarrelling with the *Zeitgeist* to expect a Molière in the fourth century B.C.

There is, however, another reason which caused these plays to be popular. It is the natural love of the people for such character-drawing as it can understand, and which by its superficiality covers a large area. It perceives broad distinctions and is happy; it requires

no more than to recognise qualities on the stage which
it has noticed in real life. For this reason Molière
and the New Comedy were equally popular: the finer
shades and better proportions of the later artist are
passed by unheeded, and the broad caricature is as
prominent in one as in the other.

This may all be considered hypercritical, for the
value of the New Comedy was just its broad, careless
imitation and knowledge of men. Its plots are as
conventional as its characters, and quite as unlikely. In
them, too, we see that the poets did not so much reason,
with Agathon, that it is probable that the improbable
will happen, as take it for granted that what has once
happened on the stage may happen again. Yet these
plays have the appearance of possible occurrences, unnecessary and improbable. They depend on a chance
meeting of all the conventional personages. There is
nothing impossible about them, just as there is nothing
impossible about the characters, but there is nothing
either probable or heroic. They exist on the stage
alone; like the *dramatis personae* they are the εἴδη of
love-affairs, in which most affairs of the sort participate
to a certain extent. It is in this way that the saying
'Menander and Nature: which of you imitated the
other?' is best explained.

In the plays of the Roman translators, the most
apparent fault is the want of concentration. This is
easily explained by the fact that the actors wore masks
which they could not change. It was therefore impossible to introduce such scenes as those in the *Scapin*
of Molière which hasten the action and do away with
unnecessary personages. Yet we cannot know how
much this is a fault peculiar to the Roman plays; for,

if the originals were slighter than the translations, this fault may have been absent from them.

These are the faults of the New Comedy considered as a part of the Drama in general. Considered by its own standard, we must allow that it stands high. The knowledge of life it shows is general, and appeals to many people; its mastery over the material at hand must have been great. Its characters are the proper characters for a drama whose merit was in its intrigue, where subtle psychology, if noticeable, is but an intrusion. Its intrigue is as varied as the knowledge of a polite Athenian would allow; robbery and love are still the bases of Comedy. And it must always be remembered that theirs was the comedy where convention was strongest. The poets struggled with the rules of the game, and where they evaded a difficulty, they gained applause. Like Japanese wrestlers, so many movements were allowed them, and the winner was he who brought off a turn with success. Here, as much as ever, in Greek literature, the spirit of a contest was paramount. The judges were conservative; he who would win must conquer by excellence in the old lines.

It is possible, however, that this estimate of the comedy falls short of the truth. There appears in the fragments a humour which has not been taken into account. It is not the magnificent devil-may-care fantasy of the Old Comedy that we can expect. That passed away with Attic liberty, and its rough laughter was replaced by an ill-natured snigger or a critical smile. Yet we have in the fragments some examples of more than polished style and neat aphorism. There is wit in some of the passages about cooks, and considerable humour in the fishmongers. The parody as a

rule seems feeble, but one travesty of the curse of
Oedipus is not bad.[1] I have quoted above a fragment
of Philippides which is almost equal to the Old Comedy
in its exaggeration. There is also a strong picture of
Dionysius Heracleotes in the *Fishers* of Menander :[2]
' A fat pig was lying on its belly . . . it had gorged
so much that it couldn't gorge long. . . . If I had my
choice this seems the only easy death, to lie on one's
back, with the fat in many folds around one, scarcely
to speak, and hardly breathing, to eat and say, " My
dissolution comes from pleasure."' But there is one
line of Menander which reaches the height of mock
heroics. It has in it the sounds of Homer, the meaning
of a nonsense verse. One cannot read it or say it over
to oneself without wondering what the author of it
could have done with a chorus and opportunity for his
feeling for language. The line runs :—

κaὶ θάλαττα βορβορώδης, ἣ μέγαν θύννον τρέφει.

It would not be an exaggeration to say that this one
line casts a new light on Menander. Whether he is
considered as a writer of good plots, who could draw
a pretty picture of the follies of humanity, or as an
observer of humanity who wrote a plot to show off
his characters, it is always thought that his merit
consisted in the quiet humour and exquisite style
of his characters and language. But if he wrote many
lines like the one above, he was a master of one of
the arts in which Aristophanes excelled. If we had
more of these lines, and more forcible descriptions of
character, we might say that he was an artist who
used great means ; but, without this evidence, we must

[1] Probably the *Oedipus* of Euripides, Eubulus 72 ; cf. Diphilus 73.
[2] Menander 21, 22, 23.

acknowledge that the ideal characters of Menander are but hypothetical, and that at present the fragments and the Roman translations remain our only guides.[1]

If it is the superficial generality of the psychology of the New Comedy that appears its fault to us, it is just that universality of its philosophy and its thought which might seem pleasant to us and true. It was this which endeared it to the Romans, just as the seeming truth of its representation of men would be accepted by the multitude. And this is only right, since it is the property of philosophy to be general, but in art a character must be true to itself, and not of necessity true in its relation to other people. No doubt the philosophy of the New Comedy is worthless as serious philosophy, but its view of life is always, in its shallow way, true, just as the virtues and vices of its characters are human and well hit off. But since a play is not a philosophical treatise, and the philosophy is in keeping with the characters, we can accept it in the New Comedy, while we reject the character-drawing as inartistic.

It would not be true to say that the New Comedy was cynical. Menander and the other poets make remarks on human nature, as it occurs to them, according to the character who utters the words. The tone of the comedy is naturally hedonist, and it would be unfair to assume that Menander consciously placed on the stage characters and actions, which he felt were wrong, with a view to the moral improvement of the

---

[1] I find that these lines are only attributed to Menander by conjecture. Athenaeus 303 c, has quoted Aeschylus, and then adds Ἀλιεῦσι without mentioning Menander. However, I have decided to let the passage remain, as there is no reason why the line should not be Menander's.

audience. He did not care for the moral effect, his
only purpose being to represent characters as he saw
them and in the positions he was pleased to see them.
It would be wrong in comedy to be anything but
pleasant, though it is certain that a moral reflection,
like a word in season, always delights the audience.
It naturally follows that we have remarks on the
wickedness of life, and on the wretchedness of exist-
ence. It is impossible that such sayings as 'Evil
communications corrupt good manners,'[1] and the many
'Reason is above all things,'[2] were anything else than
half ironical, half serious aphorisms coming with force
to the populace, who could not always see the humour
of the context. But the most striking of all the views
we have left us in the fragments is the thorough
fatalism of many of the poets, especially Menander
and Philemon. It is not the νέμεσις or ἄτη of the
tragedians which moulded the destiny of the heroes
of comedy, but a wayward, irresponsible τύχη or
αὐτόματον. This is not unnatural in a comedy where
all the events depend on an unnecessary and fortuitous
meeting of the characters, yet it is surprising to find it
expressed by the poets and the persons of the play.
'How foolish,' says Menander, in the Τίτθη, 'How
foolish are those men who raise their eyebrows[3] and
say "I'll see." You are a man, so can you see? What
can you see?[4] Even when your fortune is good you

---

[1] Men. 218. It is perhaps also a verse of Euripides. For Menander
and St. Paul, see Guizot, p. 38.

[2] A common remark, Men. 11, 69, 225, etc.

[3] Men. fr. 460, οἱ τὰς ὀφρῦς αἴροντες; Pollux, iv. 143, 145, Old
men's masks.

[4] MSS. ἄνθρωπος γὰρ ὢν | σκέψει σὺ περί του; I translate σκέψει τί;
περὶ τοῦ;

are unfortunate. For all is chance, and you are asleep when things happen to your advantage and to your disadvantage too.' And again,[1] 'Talk no more of wisdom! For man's mind is nothing, and fortune's everything—whether it be some wind divine, or some destining plan. This is what steers everything, over-turns and helps, and mortal foresight is but smoke-like and empty. Believe and blame me not. All that we think and say and do is chance; we are its devotees (ἐπιγεγραμμένοι). . . .' And again,[2] 'O Fortune, who rejoicest in all changes! thine is the blame when one who is just meets with injustice.'

That this τύχη was neither good nor bad, neither a relentless fate nor a recording angel, appears from these quotations and from another passage of Menander where he says, ' There can be injustice, it appears, even from the gods.' ' Life,' according to Alexis (34, 219), ' is like dice, which do not always fall the same way. So in life the same arrangement does not last, but is always changing.' And though the poets repeatedly complain of the power of wealth, they are continually telling us that nothing is sure on this earth, and wealth least of all.

Of the melancholy of Menander much has been said. There exist fragments, which, if they were the typical words of a poet, would, no doubt, be the index of a sad and tired temperament. 'Him, Parmeno, I call the happiest of all,' says Menander, 'who comes and sees without pain the grandeur of the world, and then departs at once to whence he came. It is in the all-

---

[1] Men. 482.
[2] Men. 590; cf. 50, 94, 144, 275, 291, 306, 355, 486, 490, 819; Apollodorus 5; Philemon 10, 111, 137; Nicos. 19, etc.

pervading sun, the stars, the rivers, clouds and fire.
All these will be ever present to you, whether you live
a hundred years or only a few, but other things greater
than these you will never see. Life is some fair,
where one comes for a short while and sees crowds and
markets, thieves, and gamblers, and frivolity.'[1] But
the evils of old age are only felt by the old man who
recites them; the very position and fate of these
characters in the drama shows the reverence with
which their sadness was treated. And the most
famous saying of all, 'Whom the gods love dies
young,'[2] is placed in the mouth of a slave who is
deceiving his old master. There is little definitely
subjective in this, nor in those passages where man
is considered the most unfortunate of animals.[3] They
are but the expression of a mood, and are followed by
the feeling of the necessity of enjoyment, even if the
world is all wrong. We can expect no system of
thought in the New Comedy other than the philosophy
of Πῖνε, παῖζε· θνητὸς ὁ βίος, ὀλίγος οὑπὶ γῇ χρόνος |
ἀθάνατος ὁ θάνατός ἐστιν, ἂν ἅπαξ τις ἀποθάνῃ.[4]
Pleasure is in the present moment, chance may change
everything, and change is disagreeable. The gods may
be, and they may not. If they are, do not fight them;
do not despise them; do not question about them.
'Do you think,' asks Menander,[5] 'that the gods have
so much time that they can deal out good and evil,
fairly, to each man, every day?' Pleasure is the god of

[1] Men. 481. Cf., generally, Wilamowitz-Moellendorf, *Hermes* xi.,
and Th. Gomperz, *ibid.*
[2] Men. 125; Plautus, *Bacch.* 4, 7, 18.
[3] Philemon 2, 3, 88, 89, 93; Men. 223.
[4] Amphis 8.   [5] Men. 174.

the New Comedy, pleasure of love and wine. 'What is this nonsense you are saying?' says a character of Alexis;[1] 'why do you babble of the Lyceum, and the Academy, and the gates of the Odeon? They are some rubbish of the philosophers, nothing of them is good. Drink, Sicon, drink; let us enjoy as long as we have life within. Come, revel, Manes; nothing is better than eating. It is your father and your mother too. Virtues, embassies, commands are empty boasts, noisy-like dreams. At an appointed time you will be turned to stone. Yours is only what you eat and drink. Everything else is ashes—Pericles and Codrus and Cimon.'

This is the philosophy of the New Comedy. It is the worldly pleasantness, the feeling of irresponsibility, half stoic, half hedonist, that we find crystallised in Horace. Optimist, Epicurean, with a tinge of Cynicism, Pessimism, and Stoicism, like the philosophical gentleman, it is not deep, but it is pleasant, and, more, it is all that is wanted.

Like the pessimistic reflections of the New Comedy are its remarks about women. Every play depended on a love-affair, and yet, 'Of all the beasts on this earth,' says Menander, 'woman is the worst.'[2] And this is not said against the courtesans, for though they are abused often enough, the largest share is given to wives. This was the ordinary Greek view, and is, naturally, more prominent in the fourth century than before. For the Greeks, while they were no longer barbarians themselves, wished to treat their woman-

---

[1] Alexis 25, Ἀσωτοδιδάσκαλος.

[2] Πολλῶν κατὰ γῆν καὶ κατὰ θάλατταν θηρίων ὄντων, | μέγιστόν ἐστι θηρίον γυνή.

kind in the old barbaric way. As they became more civilised, they must have become conscious that this was futile and wrong; they saw a force growing which they could not restrain. So, like misogynist schoolboys, they hid their fears, and, trying to show their contempt in a loud voice, proclaimed their cowardice.

Naturally the comic poets were restricted to love as the Greeks knew it, which was not the love used by novelists of the present day. To them the modern idea would have appeared meaningless, or immoral and indecent. All the plays turn on the procuring of a hetaira or on the happy result of a mistake. For the hetairae were the only available material for the poets, since they were the only women who were educated to any extent. This may seem immoral to us, but the morality of one time—this is a platitude—is immoral in another, and morality has no place in art. The New Comedy poets merely wrote of such passions as were known to their audience, and which the audience took for granted. Their views, therefore, could not seem immoral, for it is the introduction of a purer morality which is considered immoral at the time.

Then, because the morality of the New Comedy is not our morality, it has offended moralists. Because its psychology is not our idea of psychology, it does not appeal to us as literature. When we look at the characters through the conventions of our time they are untrue; when we look at them as human they have some truth. And this is because ἐὰν πάντες οἱ νόμοι ἀναιρεθῶσιν, ὁμοίως βιωσόμεθα, if all the laws were taken away, there would be no philosophers.

APPENDIX

Testimonies to Laws concerning Comedy

1. Schol. *Ar. Ach.* 67. Εὐθυμένης: οὗτός ἐστιν ὁ ἄρχων ἐφ' οὗ κατελύθη τὸ ψήφισμα τὸ περὶ τοῦ κωμῳδεῖν γραφὲν ἐπὶ Μορυχίδου· ἴσχυσεν δὲ ἐπὶ Γλαυκίνου καὶ Θεοδώρου.

2. Schol. *Ar. Ach.* 1150. Ἀντίμαχος: φασὶ γὰρ αὐτὸν γράψαι ψήφισμα ὥστε τοὺς χοροὺς μηδὲν ἐκ τῶν χορηγῶν λαμβάνειν. | ἐδόκει δὲ ὁ Ἀντίμαχος οὗτος ψήφισμα πεποιηκέναι μὴ δεῖν κωμῳδεῖν ἐξ ὀνόματος· καὶ ἐπὶ τούτῳ πολλοὶ τῶν ποιητῶν οὐ προσῆλθον ληψόμενοι τὸν καιρὸν [χορὸν] καὶ δῆλον ὅτι πολλοὶ τῶν χορευτῶν ἐπείνων· ἐχορήγει δὲ ὁ Ἀντ. τότε ὅτε εἰσήνεγκε τὸ ψήφισμα. Cf. *Diogenianus* viii. 71.

3. Schol. *Ar. Av.* 1297. Συρακόσιος: δοκεῖ δὲ καὶ ψήφισμα τεθεικέναι μὴ κωμῳδεῖσθαι ὀνομαστί τινα, ὡς Φρύνιχος ἐν Μονοτρόπῳ φησί· Ψῶρ' ἔχε Συρακόσιον, ἐπιφανὴς γὰρ αὐτῷ καὶ μέγα τύχοι. ἀφείλετο γὰρ κωμῳδεῖν οὓς ἐπεθύμουν. διὸ πικρότερον αὐτῷ προσφέρονται.

4a. Schol. *Aristidis,* p. 444, *Dind.* Ἄλλοι δὲ λέγουσιν ὅτι ἐκωμῴδουν ὀνομαστὶ τοὺς ἀνδρὰς μέχρις Εὐπόλιδος· περιεῖλε δὲ τοῦτο Ἀλκιβιάδης στρατηγὸς καὶ ῥήτωρ.

4b. Anon. ap. *Cram. Anecd.* Par. I. ψήφισμα ἔθετο Ἀλκιβιάδης μηκέτι φανερῶς ἀλλὰ συμβολικῶς κωμῳδεῖν. And he gives the story about Alcibiades ducking Eupolis in the sea after the production of the Βάπται. Cf. Platonios xxxiii. fin. xxxiv.

5. Schol. *Ar. Ra.* 404. σὺ γὰρ κατεσχίσω . . . ἔοικε
παρεμφαίνειν ὅτι λιτῶς ἤδη ἐχορηγεῖτο τοῖς ποιηταῖς. | ἐπὶ
γοῦν τοῦ Καλλίου τούτου φησὶν Ἀριστοτέλης ὅτι σύνδυο
ἔδοξε χορηγεῖν τὰ Διονύσια τοῖς τραγῳδοῖς καὶ κωμῳδοῖς ὥστε
ἦν τις καὶ παρὰ τὸν Ληναικὸν συστολὴ χρόνῳ, δι' οὗ πόλλοι
ὕστερον καθάπερ τὰς χορηγίας περιεῖλε Κινησίας. | χρόνῳ δὲ
ὕστερον οὐ πόλλῳ τινὶ καὶ καθάπαξ περιεῖλε Κιν. τὰς χορηγίας.
ἐξ οὗ καὶ Στράττις, ἐν τῷ εἰς αὐτὸν δράματι, ἔφη σκηνῇ μὲν
τοῦ χοροκτόνου Κινησίου.

6. Platonios, περὶ διαφορᾶς κωμῳδιῶν, p. xxxiv. τὰ μὲν
γὰρ ἔχοντα τὰς παραβάσεις κατ' ἐκεῖνον τὸν χρόνον ἐδιδάχθη
καθ' ὃν ὁ δῆμος ἐκράτει, τὰ δ' οὐκ ἔχοντα τῆς ἐξουσίας λοιπὸν
ἀπὸ τοῦ δήμου μεθισταμένης καὶ τῆς ὀλιγαρχίας κρατούσης.

7. Schol. *Ar. Eccl.* 102. Ἀγύρριος . . . τὸν μισθὸν δὲ
τῶν ποιητῶν συνέτεμε καὶ πρῶτος ἐκκλησιαστικὸν δέδωκεν,
κ.τ.λ. Cf. Schol. *Ar. Ran.* 362.

8. Platonios, π. δ. κ. xxxv. καὶ τὰς παραβάσεις παρῃτή-
σαντο, διὰ τὸ τοὺς χορηγοὺς ἐπιλεῖψαι χορῶν οὐκ ὄντων.

9. Schol. *Nub.* 510. νόμος ἦν Ἀθηναίοις μήπω τινὰ ἐτῶν
λ' γεγονότα μήτε δρᾶμα ἀναγιγνώσκειν ἐν θεάτρῳ μήτε
δημηγορεῖν.
Id. 530. νόμος δὲ ἦν μὴ εἰσελθεῖν τινα εἰπεῖν μήπω
τεσσαράκοντα ἔτη γεγονότα· ὡς δέ τινες, τριάκοντα.

10. Plutarch, *Bellone an pace praest. Athen.* 348 c. τῶν
δραματοποιῶν τὴν μὲν κωμῳδοποιΐαν οὕτως ἄσεμνον ἡγοῦντο
καὶ φορτικόν, ὥστε νόμος ἦν μηδένα ποιεῖν κωμῳδίας Ἀρεο-
παγίτην.

11. Schol. *Ar. Nub.* 31. καὶ τροχοῖν Ἀμυνίᾳ: τότε γὰρ
ἦρχεν Ἀμινίας Προνάπου υἱός, ἐκεῖνον οὖν ἐπισκῶψαι ἐθέλων,
παρέτρεψε τὸ Ι εἰς τὸ Υ καὶ παρεγραμμάτισε γελοίως· ἐπεὶ
παρὰ τοῖς Ἀθηναίοις ὁ νόμος φανέρως ἐκώλυε τὸν ἄρχοντα
κωμῳδεῖν.

THE CHANGE IN CHARACTER.

12. Platonios, p. xxxiv. . . . ὑπεξηρέθη τῆς κωμῳδίας τὰ χορικὰ μέλη καὶ τῶν ὑποθέσεων ὁ τρόπος μετεβλήθη. σκοποῦ γὰρ ὄντος τῆς ἀρχαίας κωμῳδίας τοῦ σκώπτειν δήμους καὶ δικαστὰς καὶ στρατηγούς, παρεὶς ὁ Ἀριστοφάνης τοῦ συνήθως ἀποσκῶψαι διὰ τὸν πολὺν φόβον, Αἴολον τὸ δρᾶμα, τὸ γραφὲν τοῖς τραγῳδοῖς, ὡς κακῶς ἔχον διασύρει. τοιοῦτος οὖν ἐστιν ὁ τῆς μέσης κωμῳδίας τύπος, οἷός ἐστιν ὁ Αἰολοσίκων Ἀριστοφάνους καὶ οἱ Ὀδυσσεῖς Κρατίνου καὶ πλεῖστα τῶν παλαιῶν δραμάτων οὔτε χορικὰ οὔτε παραβάσεις ἔχοντα . . . p. xxxv. ἡ δὲ μέση κωμῳδία ἀφῆκε τὰς τοιαύτας (personal) ὑποθέσεις, ἐπὶ δὲ τὸ σκώπτειν ἱστορίας ῥηθείσας ποιηταῖς ἦλθεν. ἀνεύθυνον γὰρ τὸ τοιοῦτον, οἷον διασύρειν Ὅμηρον εἰπόντα τι ἢ τὸν δεῖνα τῆς τραγῳδίας ποιητήν . . . ἐν δὲ τῇ μέσῃ καὶ νέᾳ κωμῳδίᾳ ἐπίτηδες τὰ προσωπεῖα πρὸς τὸ γελοιότερον ἐδημιούργησαν, δεδοικότες τοὺς Μακεδόνας, . . ἵνα μηδὲ ἐκ τύχης τινὸς ὁμοιότης προσώπου συμπέσῃ τινὶ Μακεδόνων ἄρχοντι καὶ δόξας ὁ ποιητὴς ἐκ προαιρέσεως κωμῳδεῖν δίκας ὑπόσχῃ.

13. Anon. p. xxxi. ἐπεὶ δὲ ἡ κακία προέκοπτεν, οἱ πλούσιοι καὶ οἱ ἄρχοντες μὴ βουλόμενοι κωμῳδεῖσθαι τοῦ μὲν φανερῶς κωμῳδεῖν ἐκώλυσαν, ἐκέλευσαν δὲ κρύφα, οἷον αἰνιγματωδῶς, εἶτα δὴ καὶ τοῦτο ἐκώλυσαν, καὶ πτωχοὺς ἔσκωπτον, εἰς δὲ πλουσίους καὶ ἐνδόξους οὔ. γέγονε δὲ τῆς μὲν πρώτης κωμῳδίας ἄριστος τεχνίτης οὗτος ὁ Ἀριστοφάνης, τῆς δὲ δευτέρας Πλάτων, τῆς δὲ τρίτης Μένανδρος.

13b. Schol. *Dion. Thrac.* apud *Bekker, Anecd.* p. 747, expands this account of the change and ends with—καὶ τῆς μὲν παλαιᾶς πολλοὶ γεγόνασιν, ἐπίσημος δὲ Κρατῖνος ὁ καὶ πραττόμενος. μετέσχον δέ τινος χρόνου τῆς παλαιᾶς κωμ. Εὔπολίς τε καὶ Ἀριστοφάνης, τῆς δὲ μέσης . . . ἐπίσημος . . . Πλάτων τις . . . τῆς δὲ νέας . . . Μένανδρος.

13c. Andronicus, ap. *Bekk. Anecd.* p. 1461. ἡ μὲν ἀρχαία φανερῶς ἐλέγχουσα, ἧς ἐπίσημοι Ἀριστοφάνης, Κρατῖνος,

Εὔπολις. ἡ δὲ μέση τις καὶ αἰνιγματώδης ... Πλάτων ...
ἡ δὲ νέα μηδ' ὅλως αἰνιγματώδης, πλὴν ἐπὶ δούλων καὶ ξένων,
ἧς ἐπίσημος Μένανδρος καὶ παρὰ Ῥωμαίοις Τερέντιος καὶ
Πλαῦτος.

13d. Anon. *Cramer. Anecd.* Par. I. 3 *seq.*, after what is
quoted above, 4b. Τότε δὴ αὐτός τε Εὔπολις καὶ Κρατῖνος
καὶ Φερεκράτης καὶ Πλάτων καὶ Ἀριστοφάνης αὐτὸς τὰ
συμβολικῶς μετεχειρίσατο σκώμματα, ἢ δὴ δεύτερα κωμῳδία
ἐλέγετο, μέχρις οὗ μηδὲ συμβολικῶς ἐθελόντων τῶν πολιτῶν
σκώπτεσθαι, εἰς δούλους μόνους καὶ ξένους ἔσκωπτον, ἡ δὲ
τρίτη ἦν κωμῳδία, αὐξηθεῖσα ἐπὶ Μενάνδρου καὶ Φιλήμονος.

13e. Joannes Tzetzes, l. 79.
> πρώτης μὲν ἦν ἴδιον ἐμφανὴς ψόγος·
> ἧς ἦν κατάρξας εὑρετὴς Σουσαρίων.
> τῆς δευτέρας ἦν ὁ ψόγος κεκρυμμένος·
> ἧς ἦν Κρατῖνος, Εὔπολις, Φερεκράτης,
> Ἀριστοφάνης, Ἕρμιππός τε καὶ Πλάτων.
> καὶ τῆς τρίτης ἦν ὁ ψόγος κεκρυμμένος,
> πλὴν κατὰ δούλων καὶ ξένων καὶ βαρβάρων·
> ἧς ἦν Μένανδρος ἐργάτης καὶ Φιλήμων.

14. Anon. p. xxxii. Τῆς κωμῳδίας τὸ μέν ἐστιν ἀρχαῖον,
τὸ δέ νέον [τὸ δὲ μέσον.] τῆς δὲ νέας διαφέρει ἡ παλαιὰ κωμ.
χρόνῳ, διαλέκτῳ, ὕλῃ, μέτρῳ, διασκευῇ. χρόνῳ μὲν, καθὸ ἡ
μὲν νέα ἐπὶ Ἀλεξάνδρου, ἡ δὲ παλαιὰ ἐπὶ τῶν Πελοποννησια-
κῶν εἶχε τὴν ἀκμήν. διαλέκτῳ δὲ, καθὸ ἡ μὲν νέα τὸ σαφέσ-
τερον ἔχει, τῇ νέᾳ κεχρημένη Ἀτθίδι, ἡ δὲ παλαιὰ τὸ δεινὸν
καὶ ὑψηλὸν τοῦ λέγειν, ἐνίοτε δὲ ἐπιτηδεύει καὶ λέξεις τινάς.
ὕλῃ δε, <... μέτρῳ δὲ, > καθὸ ἡ μὲν νέα ... ἰαμβικὸν ...,
ἐν δὲ τῇ παλαιᾷ πολυμετρία ... διασκευῇ δὲ, ὅτι ἐν τῇ μὲν νέᾳ
χόρου οὐκ ἔδει, ἐν ἐκείνῃ δὲ δεῖ. καὶ αὐτὴ δὲ ἡ παλαιὰ ἑαυτῆς
διαφέρει. Here follows a contrast between Susario and
Cratinus.

15. *Id. fin.* ὁ μέντοι γε Ἀριστοφάνης μεθοδεύσας τεχνι-

κώτερον τῆς μεθ' ἑαυτοῦ τὴν κωμῳδίαν, ἐνέλαμψεν ἐν ἅπασιν,
ἐπίσημος ὀφθεὶς οὕτω, καὶ οὕτω πᾶσαν κωμῳδίαν ἐμελέτησε.
καὶ γὰρ τὸ τούτου δρᾶμα ὁ Πλοῦτος νεωτερίζει κατὰ τὸ
πλάσμα. τὴν τὲ γὰρ ὑπόθεσιν [οὐκ] ἀληθῆ ἔχει καὶ χορῶν
ἐστέρηται· ὅπερ τῆς νέας ὑπῆρχε κωμῳδίας.

[οὐκ] I seclude ; cf. App. 16.

15b. *Life of Aristophanes*, xxxvii, xxxviii. ἐγένετο δὲ καὶ
αἴτιος ζήλου τοῖς νέοις κωμικοῖς, λέγω δὲ Φιλήμονι καὶ
Μενάνδρῳ. ψηφίσματος γὰρ γενομένου χορηγοῦ [χορηγικοῦ,
Mein.], ὥστε μὴ ὀνομαστὶ κωμῳδεῖν τινα, καὶ τῶν χορηγῶν
οὐκ ἀντεχόντων πρὸς τὸ χορηγεῖν, καὶ παντάπασιν ἐκλελοιπυίας
τῆς ὕλης τῶν κωμῳδιῶν διὰ τούτων αὐτῶν, αἴτιον γὰρ κωμῳδίας
τὸ σκώπτειν τινάς, ἔγραψε [κωμῳδίας τινὰς] Κώκαλον, ἐν ᾧ
εἰσάγει φθορὰν καὶ ἀναγνωρισμὸν καὶ τἄλλα πάντα ἃ ἐζήλωσε
Μένανδρος. πάλιν δέ, ἐκλελοιπότος καὶ τοῦ χορηγεῖν, τὸν
Πλοῦτον γράψας εἰς τὸ διαπαύεσθαι τὰ σκηνικὰ πρόσωπα καὶ
μετεσκευάσθαι, ἐπιγράφει χοροῦ, φθεγγόμενος ἐν ἐκείνοις ἃ
καὶ ὁρῶμεν τοὺς νέους ἐπιγράφοντας οὕτω ζήλῳ 'Αριστο-
φάνους.

16. Anon. p. xxx. Τῆς δὲ μέσης κωμῳδίας οἱ ποιηταὶ
πλάσματος οὐχ ἥψαντο ποιητικοῦ, διὰ δὲ τῆς συνήθους ἰόντες
λαλιᾶς λογικὰς ἔχουσι τὰς ἀρετάς, ὥστε σπάνιον ποιητικὸν
εἶναι χαρακτῆρα παρ' αὐτοῖς. κατασχολοῦνται δὲ πάντες περὶ
τὰς ὑποθέσεις. τῆς μὲν οὖν μέσης κωμῳδίας εἰσὶ ποιηταὶ νζ',
καὶ τούτων δράματα χιζ'. τούτων δέ εἰσιν ἀξιολογώτατοι
'Αντιφάνης καὶ "Αλεξις . . . *Life of Antiphanes* . . . τῆς δὲ
νέας κωμῳδίας . . . ἀξιολογώτατοι . . . Φιλήμων, Μένανδρος,
Δίφιλος, Φιλιππίδης, Ποσείδιππος, 'Απολλόδωρος.